The Voice of the

An Introduction to the Twentieth Century

Gerald Stanley Lee

Alpha Editions

This edition published in 2024

ISBN : 9789362993359

Design and Setting By
Alpha Editions
www.alphaedis.com
Email - info@alphaedis.com

Contents

PART ONE
THE MEN BEHIND THE MACHINES

I

MACHINES. AS SEEN FROM A MEADOW

It would be difficult to find anything in the encyclopedia that would justify the claim that we are about to make, or anything in the dictionary. Even a poem—which is supposed to prove anything with a little of nothing—could hardly be found to prove it; but in this beginning hour of the twentieth century there are not a few of us—for the time at least allowed to exist upon the earth—who are obliged to say (with Luther), "Though every tile on the roundhouse be a devil, we cannot say otherwise—the locomotive is beautiful."

As seen when one is looking at it as it is, and is not merely using it.

As seen from a meadow.

We had never thought to fall so low as this, or that the time would come when we would feel moved—all but compelled, in fact—to betray to a cold and discriminating world our poor, pitiful, one-adjective state.

We do not know why a locomotive is beautiful. We are perfectly aware that it ought not to be. We have all but been ashamed of it for being beautiful—and of ourselves. We have attempted all possible words upon it—the most complimentary and worthy ones we know—words with the finer resonance in them, and the air of discrimination the soul loves. We cannot but say that several of these words from time to time have seemed almost satisfactory to our ears. They seem satisfactory also for general use in talking with people, and for introducing locomotives in conversation; but the next time we see a locomotive coming down the track, there is no help for us. We quail before the headlight of it. The thunder of its voice is as the voice of the hurrying people. Our little row of adjectives is vanished. All adjectives are vanished. They are as one.

Unless the word "beautiful" is big enough to make room for a glorious, imperious, world-possessing, world-commanding beauty like this, we are no longer its disciples. It is become a play word. It lags behind truth. Let it be shut in with its rim of hills—the word beautiful—its show of sunsets and its bouquets and its doilies and its songs of birds. We are seekers for a new word. It is the first hour of the twentieth century. If the hill be beautiful, so is the locomotive that conquers a hill. So is the telephone, piercing a thousand sunsets north to south, with the sound of a voice. The night is not more beautiful, hanging its shadow over the city, than the electric spark pushing the night one side, that the city may behold itself; and the hour is at hand—is even now upon us—when not the sun itself shall be more beautiful to men than the telegraph stopping the sun in the midst of its high heaven, and holding it there, while the will of a child to another child ticks round the earth. "Time shall be folded up as a scroll," saith the voice of Man, my Brother. "The spaces between the hills, to ME," saith the Voice, "shall be as though they were not."

The voice of man, my brother, is a new voice.

It is the voice of the machines.

II

AS SEEN THROUGH A HATCHWAY

In its present importance as a factor in life and a modifier of its conditions, the machine is in every sense a new and unprecedented fact. The machine has no traditions. The only way to take a traditional stand with regard to life or the representation of life to-day, is to leave the machine out. It has always been left out. Leaving it out has made little difference. Only a small portion of the people of the world have had to be left out with it.

Not to see poetry in the machinery of this present age, is not to see poetry in the life of the age. It is not to believe in the age.

The first fact a man encounters in this modern world, after his mother's face, is the machine. The moment be begins to think outwards, he thinks toward a machine. The bed he lies in was sawed and planed by a machine, or cast in a foundry. The windows he looks out of were built in mills. His knife and fork were made by steam. His food has come through rollers and wheels. The water he drinks is pumped to him by engines. The ice in it was frozen by a factory and the cloth of the clothes he wears was flashed together by looms.

The machine does not end here. When he grows to years of discretion and looks about him to choose a place for himself in life, he finds that that place must come to him out of a machine. By the side of a machine of one sort or another, whether it be of steel rods and wheels or of human beings' souls, he must find his place in the great whirling system of the order of mortal lives, and somewhere in the system—that is, the Machine—be the ratchet, drive-wheel, belt, or spindle under infinite space, ordained for him to be from the beginning of the world.

The moment he begins to think, a human being finds himself facing a huge, silent, blue-and-gold something called the universe, the main fact of which must be to him that it seems to go without him very well, and that he must drop into the place that comes, whatever it may be, and hold on as he loves his soul, or forever be left behind. He learns before many years that this great machine shop of a globe, turning solemnly its days and nights, where he has wandered for a life, will hardly be inclined to stop—to wait perchance—to ask him what he wants to be, or how this life of his shall get itself said. He looks into the Face of Circumstance. (Sometimes it is the Fist of Circumstance.) The Face of Circumstance is a silent face. It points to the machine. He looks into the faces of his fellow-men, hurrying past him night and day,—miles of streets of them. They, too, have looked into the Face of Circumstance. It pointed to the Machine. They show it in their faces. Some of them show it in their gait. The Machine closes around him, with its vast insistent murmur, million-peopled and full of laughs and cries. He listens to it as to the roar of all Being.

He listens to the Machine's prophet. "All men," says Political Economy, "may be roughly divided as attaching themselves to one or the other of three great classes of activity—production, consumption or distribution."

The number of persons who are engaged in production outside of association with machinery, if they could be gathered together in one place, would be an exceedingly small and strange and uncanny band of human beings. They would be visited by all the world as curiosities.

The number of persons who are engaged in distribution outside of association with machinery is equally insignificant. Except for a few peddlers, distribution is hardly anything else but machinery.

The number of persons who are engaged in consumption outside of association with machinery is equally insignificant. So far as consumption is concerned, any passing freight train, if it could be stopped and examined on its way to New York, would be found to be loaded with commodities, the most important part of which, from the coal up, have been produced by one set of machines to be consumed by another set of machines.

So omnipresent and masterful and intimate with all existence have cogs and wheels and belts become, that not a civilized man could be found on the globe to-day, who, if all the machines that have helped him to live this single year of 1906 could be gathered or piled around him where he stands, would be able, for the machines piled high around his life, to see the sky—to be sure there was a sky. It is then his privilege, looking up at this horizon of steel and iron and running belts, to read in a paper book the literary definition of what this heaven is, that spreads itself above him, and above the world, walled in forever with its irrevocable roar of wheels.

"No inspiring emotions," says the literary definition, "ideas or conceptions can possibly be connected with machinery—or ever will be."

What is to become of a world roofed in with machines for the rest of its natural life, and of the people who will have to live under the roof of machines, the literary definition does not say. It is not the way of literary definitions. For a time at least we feel assured that we, who are the makers of definitions, are poetically and personally safe. Can we not live behind the ramparts of our books? We take comfort with the medallions of poets and the shelves that sing around us. We sit by our library fires, the last nook of poetry. Beside our gates the great crowding chimneys lift themselves. Beneath our windows herds of human beings, flocking through the din, in the dark of the morning and the dark of the night, go marching to their fate. We have done what we could. Have we not defined poetry? Is it nothing to have laid the boundary line of beauty?... The huge, hurrying, helpless world in its belts and spindles—the people who are going to be obliged to live in it when the present tense has spoiled it a little more—all this—the great strenuous problem—the defense of beauty, the saving of its past, the forging of its future, the welding of it with life-all these?... Pull down the blinds, Jeems. Shut out the noises of the street. A little longer ... the low singing to ourselves. Then darkness. The wheels and the din above our graves shall be as the passing of silence.

Is it true that, in a few years more, if a man wants the society of his kind, he will have to look down through a hatchway? Or that, if he wants to be happy, he will have to stand on it and look away? I do not know. I only know how it is now.

They stay not in their hold

These stokers,

Stooping to hell

To feed a ship.

Below the ocean floors,

Before their awful doors

Bathed in flame,

I hear their human lives

Drip—drip.

Through the lolling aisles of comrades

In and out of sleep,

Troops of faces

To and fro of happy feet,

They haunt my eyes.

Their murky faces beckon me

From the spaces of the coolness of the sea

Their fitful bodies away against the skies.

III

SOULS OF MACHINES

It does not make very much difference to the machines whether there is poetry in them or not. It is a mere abstract question to the machines.

It is not an abstract question to the people who are under the machines. Men who are under things want to know what the things are for, and they want to know what they are under them for. It is a very live, concrete, practical question whether there is, or can be, poetry in machinery or not. The fate of society turns upon it.

There seems to be nothing that men can care for, whether in this world or the next, or that they can do, or have, or hope to have, which is not bound up, in our modern age, with machinery. With the fate of machinery it stands or falls. Modern religion is a machine. If the characteristic vital power and spirit of the modern age is organization, and it cannot organize in its religion, there is little to be hoped for in religion. Modern education is a machine. If the principle of machinery is a wrong and inherently uninspired principle— if because a machine is a machine no great meaning can be expressed by it, and no great result accomplished by it—there is little to be hoped for in modern education.

Modern government is a machine. The more modern a government is, the more the machine in it is emphasized. Modern trade is a machine. It is made up of (1) corporations—huge machines employing machines, and (2) of trusts—huge machines that control machines that employ machines. Modern charity is a machine for getting people to help each other. Modern society is a machine for getting them to enjoy each other. Modern literature is a machine for supplying ideas. Modern journalism is a machine for distributing them; and modern art is a machine for supplying the few, very few, things that are left that other machines cannot supply.

Both in its best and worst features the characteristic, inevitable thing that looms up in modern life over us and around us, for better or worse, is the machine. We may whine poetry at it, or not. It makes little difference to the machine. We may not see what it is for. It has come to stay. It is going to stay until we do see what it is for. We cannot move it. We cannot go around it. We cannot destroy it. We are born in the machine. A man cannot move the place he is born in. We breathe the machine. A man cannot go around what he breathes, any more than he can go around himself. He cannot destroy what he breathes, even by destroying himself. If there cannot be poetry in machinery—that is if there is no beautiful and glorious interpretation of machinery for our modern life—there cannot be poetry in anything in modern life. Either the machine is the door of the future, or it stands and mocks at us where the door ought to be. If we who have made machines cannot make our machines mean something, we ourselves are meaningless, the great blue-and-gold machine above our lives is meaningless, the winds that blow down upon us from it are empty winds, and the lights that lure us in it are pictures of darkness. There is one question that confronts and undergirds our whole modern civilization. All other questions are a part of it. Can a Machine Age have a soul?

If we can find a great hope and a great meaning for the machine-idea in its simplest form, for machinery itself—that is, the machines of steel and flame that minister to us—it will be possible to find a great hope for our other machines. If we cannot use the machines we have already mastered to hope with, the less we hope from our other machines—our spirit-machines, the machines we have not mastered—the better. In taking the stand that there is poetry in machinery, that inspiring ideas and emotions can be and will be connected with machinery, we are taking a stand for the continued existence of modern religion—(in all reverence) the God-machine; for modern education—the man-machine; for modern government—the crowd-machine; for modern art—the machine in which the crowd lives.

If inspiring ideas cannot be connected with a machine simply because it is a machine, there is not going to be anything left in this modern world to connect inspiring ideas with.

Johnstown haunts me—the very memory of it. Flame and vapor and shadow—like some huge, dim face of Labor, it lifts itself dumbly and looks at me. I suppose, to some it is but a wraith of rusty vapor, a mist of old iron, sparks floating from a chimney, while a train sweeps past. But to me, with its spires of smoke and its towers of fire, it is as if a great door had been opened and I had watched a god, down in the wonder of real things—in the act of making an earth. I am filled with childhood—and a kind of strange, happy terror. I struggle to wonder my way out. Thousands of railways—after this— bind Johnstown to me; miles of high, narrow, steel-built streets—the whole world lifting itself mightily up, rolling itself along, turning itself over on a great steel pivot, down in Pennsylvania—for its days and nights. I am whirled away from it as from a vision. I am as one who has seen men lifting their souls up in a great flame and laying down floors on a star. I have stood and watched, in the melting-down place, the making and the welding place of the bones of the world.

It is the object of this present writing to search out a world—a world a man can live in. If he cannot live in this one, let him know it and make one. If he can, let him face it. If the word YES cannot be written across the world once more—written across this year of the world in the roar of its vast machines— we want to know it. We cannot quite see the word YES—sometimes, huddled behind our machines. But we hear it sometimes. We know we hear it. It is stammered to us by the machines themselves.

IV

POETS

When, standing in the midst of the huge machine-shop of our modern life, we are informed by the Professor of Poetics that machinery—the thing we do our living with—is inevitably connected with ideas practical and utilitarian—at best intellectual—that "it will always be practically impossible to make poetry out of it, to make it appeal to the imagination," we refer the question to the real world, to the real spirit we know exists in the real world.

Expectancy is the creed of the twentieth century.

Expectancy, which was the property of poets in the centuries that are now gone by, is the property to-day of all who are born upon the earth.

The man who is not able to draw a distinction between the works of John Milton and the plays of Shakespeare, but who expects something of the age he lives in, comes nearer to being a true poet than any writer of verses can ever expect to be who does not expect anything of this same age he lives in—not even verses. Expectancy is the practice of poetry. It is poetry caught in the act. Though the whole world be lifting its voice, and saying in the same breath that poetry is dead, this same world is living in the presence of more poetry, and more kinds of poetry, than men have known on the earth before, even in the daring of their dreams.

Pessimism has always been either literary—the result of not being in the real world enough—or genuine and provincial—the result of not being in enough of the real world.

If we look about in this present day for a suitable and worthy expectancy to make an age out of, or even a poem out of, where shall we look for it? In the literary definition? the historical argument? the minor poet?

The poet of the new movement shall not be discovered talking with the doctors, or defining art in the schools, nor shall he be seen at first by peerers in books. The passer-by shall see him, perhaps, through the door of a foundry at night, a lurid figure there, bent with labor, and humbled with labor, but with the fire from the heart of the earth playing upon his face. His hands—innocent of the ink of poets, of the mere outsides of things—shall be beautiful with the grasp of the thing called life—with the grim, silent, patient creating of life. He shall be seen living with retorts around him, loomed over by machines—shadowed by weariness—to the men about him half comrade, half monk—going in and out among them silently, with some secret glory in his heart.

If literary men—so called—knew the men who live with machines, who are putting their lives into them—inventors, engineers and brakemen—as well as they know Shakespeare and Milton and the Club, there would be no difficulty about finding a great meaning—*i. e.*, a great hope or great poetry—in machinery. The real problem that stands in the way of poetry in machinery is not literary, nor æsthetic. It is sociological. It is in getting people to notice that an engineer is a gentleman and a poet.

V

GENTLEMEN

The truest definition of a gentleman is that he is a man who loves his work. This is also the truest definition of a poet. The man who loves his work is a poet because he expresses delight in that work. He is a gentleman because his delight in that work makes him his own employer. No matter how many men are over him, or how many men pay him, or fail to pay him, he stands under the wide heaven the one man who is master of the earth. He is the one infallibly overpaid man on it. The man who loves his work has the single thing the world affords that can make a man free, that can make him his own employer, that admits him to the ranks of gentlemen, that pays him, or is rich enough to pay him, what a gentleman's work is worth.

The poets of the world are the men who pour their passions into it, the men who make the world over with their passions. Everything that these men touch, as with some strange and immortal joy from out of them, has the thrill of beauty in it, and exultation and wonder. They cannot have it otherwise even if they would. A true man is the autobiography of some great delight mastering his heart for him, possessing his brain, making his hands beautiful.

Looking at the matter in this way, in proportion to the number employed there are more gentlemen running locomotives to-day than there are teaching in colleges. In proportion as we are more creative in creating machines at present than we are in creating anything else there are more poets in the mechanical arts than there are in the fine arts; and while many of the men who are engaged in the machine-shops can hardly be said to be gentlemen (that is, they would rather be preachers or lawyers), these can be more than offset by the much larger proportion of men in the fine arts, who, if they were gentlemen in the truest sense, would turn mechanics at once; that is, they would do the thing they were born to do, and they would respect that thing, and make every one else respect it.

While the definition of a poet and a gentleman—that he is a man who loves his work—might appear to make a new division of society, it is a division that already exists in the actual life of the world, and constitutes the only literal aristocracy the world has ever had.

It may be set down as a fundamental principle that, no matter how prosaic a man may be, or how proud he is of having been born upon this planet with poetry all left out of him, it is the very essence of the most hard and practical man that, as regards the one uppermost thing in his life, the thing that reveals the power in him, he is a poet in spite of himself, and whether he knows it or not.

So long as the thing a man works with is a part of an inner ideal to him, so long as he makes the thing he works with express that ideal, the heat and the glow and the lustre and the beauty and the unconquerableness of that man, and of that man's delight, shall be upon all that he does. It shall sing to heaven. It shall sing to all on earth who overhear heaven.

Every man who loves his work, who gets his work and his ideal connected, who makes his work speak out the heart of him, is a poet. It makes little difference what he says about it. In proportion as he has power with a thing; in proportion as he makes the thing—be it a bit of color, or a fragment of flying sound, or a word, or a wheel, or a throttle—in proportion as he makes the thing fulfill or express what he wants it to fulfill or express, he is a poet. All heaven and earth cannot make him otherwise.

That the inventor is in all essential respects a poet toward the machine that he has made, it would be hard to deny. That, with all the apparent prose that piles itself about his machine, the machine is in all essential respects a poem to him, who can question? Who has ever known an inventor, a man with a passion in his hands, without feeling toward him as he feels toward a poet? Is it nothing to us to know that men are living now under the same sky with us, hundreds of them (their faces haunt us on the street), who would all but die, who are all but dying now, this very moment, to make a machine live,—martyrs of valves and wheels and of rivets and retorts, sleepless, tireless, unconquerable men?

To know an inventor the moment of his triumph,—the moment when, working his will before him, the machine at last, resistless, silent, massive pantomime of a life, offers itself to the gaze of men's souls and the needs of their bodies,—to know an inventor at all is to know that at a moment like this a chord is touched in him strange and deep, soft as from out of all eternity. The melody that Homer knew, and that Dante knew, is his also, with the grime upon his hands, standing and watching it there. It is the same song that from pride to pride and joy to joy has been singing through the hearts of The Men Who Make, from the beginning of the world. The thing that was not, that now is, after all the praying with his hands … iron and wood and rivet and cog and wheel—is it not more than these to him standing before it there? It is the face of matter—who does not know it?—answering the face of the man, whispering to him out of the dust of the earth.

What is true of the men who make the machines is equally true of the men who live with them. The brakeman and the locomotive engineer and the mechanical engineer and the sailor all have the same spirit. Their days are invested with the same dignity and aspiration, the same unwonted enthusiasm, and self-forgetfulness in the work itself. They begin their lives as boys dreaming of the track, or of cogs and wheels, or of great waters.

As I stood by the track the other night, Michael the switchman was holding the road for the nine o'clock freight, with his faded flag, and his grim brown pipe, and his wooden leg. As it rumbled by him, headlight, clatter, and smoke, and whirl, and halo of the steam, every brakeman backing to the wind, lying on the air, at the jolt of the switch, started, as at some greeting out of the dark, and turned and gave the sign to Michael. All of the brakemen gave it. Then we watched them, Michael and I, out of the roar and the hiss of their splendid cloud, their flickering, swaying bodies against the sky, flying out to the Night, until there was nothing but a dull red murmur and the falling of smoke.

Michael hobbled back to his mansion by the rails. He put up the foot that was left from the wreck, and puffed and puffed. He had been a brakeman himself.

Brakemen are prosaic men enough, no doubt, in the ordinary sense, but they love a railroad as Shakespeare loved a sonnet. It is not given to brakemen, as it is to poets, to show to the world as it passes by that their ideals are beautiful. They give their lives for them,—hundreds of lives a year. These lives may be sordid lives looked at from the outside, but mystery, danger, surprise, dark cities, and glistening lights, roar, dust, and water, and death, and life,—these play their endless spell upon them. They love the shining of the track. It is wrought into the very fibre of their being.

Years pass and years, and still more years. Who shall persuade the brakemen to leave the track? They never leave it. I shall always see them—on their flying footboards beneath the sky—swaying and rocking—still swaying and rocking—to Eternity.

They are men who live down through to the spirit and the poetry of their calling. It is the poetry of the calling that keeps them there.

Most of us in this mortal life are allowed but our one peephole in the universe, that we may see IT withal; but if we love it enough and stand close to it enough, we breathe the secret and touch in our lives the secret that throbs through it all.

For a man to have an ideal in this world, for a man to know what an ideal is, even though nothing but a wooden leg shall come of it, and a life in a switch-house, and the signal of comrades whirling by, this also is to have lived.

The fact that the railroad has the same fascination for the railroad man that the sea has for the sailor is not a mere item of interest pertaining to human nature. It is a fact that pertains to the art of the present day, and to the future of its literature. It is as much a symbol of the art of a machine age as the man Ulysses is a symbol of the art of an heroic age.

That it is next to impossible to get a sailor, with all his hardships, to turn his back upon the sea is a fact a great many thousand years old. We find it accounted for not only in the observation and experience of men, but in their art. It was rather hard for them to do it at first (as with many other things), but even the minor poets have admitted the sea into poetry. The sea was allowed in poetry before mountains were allowed in it. It has long been an old story. When the sailor has grown too stiff to climb the masts he mends sails on the decks. Everybody understands—even the commonest people and the minor poets understand—why it is that a sailor, when he is old and bent and obliged to be a landsman to die, does something that holds him close to the sea. If he has a garden, he hoes where he can see the sails. If he must tend flowers, he plants them in an old yawl, and when he selects a place for his grave, it is where surges shall be heard at night singing to his bones. Every one appreciates a fact like this. There is not a passenger on the Empire State Express, this moment, being whirled to the West, who could not write a sonnet on it,—not a man of them who could not sit down in his seat, flying through space behind the set and splendid hundred-guarding eyes of the engineer, and write a poem on a dead sailor buried by the sea. A crowd on the street could write a poem on a dead sailor (that is, if they were sure he was dead), and now that sailors enough have died in the course of time to bring the feeling of the sea over into poetry, sailors who are still alive are allowed in it. It remains to be seen how many wrecks it is going to take, lists of killed and wounded, fatally injured, columns of engineers dying at their posts, to penetrate the spiritual safe where poets are keeping their souls to-day, untouched of the world, and bring home to them some sense of the adventure and quiet splendor and unparalleled expressiveness of the engineer's life. He is a man who would rather be without a life (so long as he has his nerve) than to have to live one without an engine, and when he climbs down from the old girl at last, to continue to live at all, to him, is to linger where she is. He watches the track as a sailor watches the sea. He spends his old age in the roundhouse. With the engines coming in and out, one always sees him sitting in the sun there until he dies, and talking with them. Nothing can take him away.

Does any one know an engineer who has not all but a personal affection for his engine, who has not an ideal for his engine, who holding her breath with his will does not put his hand upon the throttle of that ideal and make that ideal say something? Woe to the poet who shall seek to define down or to sing away that ideal. In its glory, in darkness or in day, we are hid from death. It is the protection of life. The engineer who is not expressing his whole soul in his engine, and in the aisles of souls behind him, is not worthy to place his hand upon an engine's throttle. Indeed, who is he—this man—that this awful privilege should be allowed to him, that he should dare to touch the motor nerve of her, that her mighty forty-mile-an-hour muscles should be the slaves of the fingers of a man like this, climbing the hills for him, circling the globe for him? It is impossible to believe that an engineer—a man who with a single touch sends a thousand tons of steel across the earth as an empty wind can go, or as a pigeon swings her wings, or as a cloud sets sail in the west—does not mean something by it, does not love to do it because he means something by it. If ever there was a poet, the engineer is a poet. In his dumb and mighty, thousand-horizoned brotherhood, hastener of men from the ends of the earth that they may be as one, I always see him,—ceaseless—tireless—flying past sleep—out through the Night—thundering down the edge of the world, into the Dawn.

Who am I that it should be given to me to make a word on my lips to speak, or to make a thing that shall be beautiful with my hands—that I should stand by my brother's life and gaze on his trembling track—and not feel what the engine says as it plunges past, about the man in the cab? What matters it that he is a wordless man, that he wears not his heart in a book? Are not the bell and the whistle and the cloud of steam, and the rush, and the peering in his eyes words enough? They are the signals of this man's life beckoning to my life. Standing in his engine there, making every wheel of that engine thrill to his will, he is the priest of wonder to me, and of the terror of the splendor of the beauty of power. The train is the voice of his life. The sound of its coming is a psalm of strength. It is as the singing a man would sing who felt his hand on the throttle of things. The engine is a soul to me—soul of the quiet face thundering past—leading its troop of glories echoing along the hills, telling it to the flocks in the fields and the birds in the air, telling it to the trees and the buds and the little, trembling growing things, that the might of the spirit of man has passed that way.

If an engine is to be looked at from the point of view of the man who makes it and who knows it best; if it is to be taken, as it has a right to be taken, in the nature of things, as being an expression of the human spirit, as being that man's way of expressing the human spirit, there shall be no escape for the children of this present world, from the wonder and beauty in it, and the strong delight in it that shall hem life in, and bound it round on every side. The idealism and passion and devotion and poetry in an engineer, in the feeling he has about his machine, the power with which that machine expresses that feeling, is one of the great typical living inspirations of this modern age, a fragment of the new apocalypse, vast and inarticulate and far and faint to us, but striving to reach us still, now from above, and now from below, and on every side of life. It is as though the very ground itself should speak,—speak to our poor, pitiful, unspiritual, matter-despising souls,—should command them to come forth, to live, to gaze into the heart of matter for the heart of God. It is so that the very dullest of us, standing among our machines, can hardly otherwise than guess the coming of some vast surprise,—the coming of the day when, in the very rumble of the world, our sons and daughters shall prophesy, and our young men shall see visions, and our old men shall dream dreams. It cannot be uttered. I do not dare to say it. What it means to our religion and to our life and to our art, this great athletic uplift of the world, I do not know. I only know that so long as the fine arts, in an age like this, look down on the mechanical arts there shall be no fine arts. I only know that so long as the church worships the laborer's God, but does not reverence labor, there shall be no religion in it for men to-day, and none for women and children to-morrow. I only know that so long as there is no poet amongst us, who can put himself into a word, as this man, my brother the engineer, is putting himself into his engine, the engine shall remove mountains, and the word of the poet shall not; it shall be buried beneath the mountains. I only know that so long as we have more preachers who can be hired to stop preaching or to go into life insurance than we have engineers who can be hired to leave their engines, inspiration shall be looked for more in engine cabs than in pulpits,—the vestibule trains shall say deeper things than sermons say. In the rhythm of the anthem of them singing along the rails, we shall find again the worship we have lost in church, the worship we fain would find in the simpered prayers and paid praises of a thousand choirs,—the worship of the creative spirit, the beholding of a fragment of creation morning, the watching of the delight of a man in the delight of God,—in the first and last delight of God. I have made a vow in my heart. I shall not enter a pulpit to speak, unless every word have the joy of God and of fathers and mothers in it. And so long as men are more creative and godlike in engines than they are in sermons, I listen to engines.

Would to God it were otherwise. But so it shall be with all of us. So it cannot but be. Not until the day shall come when this wistful, blundering church of ours, loved with exceeding great and bitter love, with all her proud and solitary towers, shall turn to the voices of life sounding beneath her belfries in the street, shall she be worshipful; not until the love of all life and the love of all love is her love, not until all faces are her faces, not until the face of the engineer peering from his cab, sentry of a thousand souls, is beautiful to her, as an altar cloth is beautiful or a stained glass window is beautiful, shall the church be beautiful. That day is bound to come. If the church will not do it with herself, the great rough hand of the world shall do it with the church. That day of the new church shall be known by men because it will be a day in which all worship shall be gathered into her worship, in which her holy house shall be the comradeship of all delights and of all masteries under the sun, and all the masteries and all the delights shall be laid at her feet.

VI

PROPHETS

The world follows the creative spirit. Where the spirit is creating, the strong and the beautiful flock. If the creative spirit is not in poetry, poetry will call itself something else. If it is not in the church, religion will call itself something else. It is the business of a living religion, not to wish that the age it lives in were some other age, but to tell what the age is for, and what every man born in it is for. A church that can see only what a few of the men born in an age are for, can help only a few. If a church does not believe in a particular man more than he believes in himself, the less it tries to do for him the better. If a church does not believe in a man's work as he believes in it, does not see some divine meaning and spirit in it and give him honor and standing and dignity for the divine meaning in it; if it is a church in which labor is secretly despised and in which it is openly patronized, in which a man has more honor for working feebly with his brain than for working passionately and perfectly with his hands, it is a church that stands outside of life. It is excommunicated by the will of Heaven and the nature of things, from the only Communion that is large enough for a man to belong to or for a God to bless.

If there is one sign rather than another of religious possibility and spiritual worth in the men who do the world's work with machines to-day, it is that these men are never persuaded to attend a church that despises that work.

Symposiums on how to reach the masses are pitiless irony. There is no need for symposiums. It is an open secret. It cries upon the house-tops. It calls above the world in the Sabbath bells. A church that believes less than the world believes shall lose its leadership in the world. "Why should I pay pew rent," says the man who sings with his hands, "to men who do not believe in me, to worship, with men who do not believe in me, a God that does not believe in me?" If heaven itself (represented as a rich and idle place,—seats free in the evening) were opened to the true laboring man on the condition that he should despise his hands by holding palms in them, he would find some excuse for staying away. He feels in no wise different with regard to his present life. "Unless your God," says the man who sings with his hands, to those who pity him and do him good,—"unless your God is a God I can worship in a factory, He is not a God I care to worship in a church."

Behold it is written: The church that does not delight in these men and in what these men are for, as much as the street delights in them, shall give way to the street. The street is more beautiful. If the street is not let into the church, it shall sweep over the church and sweep around it, shall pile the floors of its strength upon it, above it. From the roofs of labor—radiant and beautiful labor—shall men look down upon its towers. Only a church that believes more than the world believes shall lead the world. It always leads the world. It cannot help leading it. The religion that lives in a machine age, and that cannot see and feel, and make others see and feel, the meaning of that machine age, is a religion which is not worthy of us. It is not worthy of our machines. One of the machines we have made could make a better religion than this. Even now, almost everywhere in almost every town or city where one goes, if one will stop or look up or listen, one hears the chimneys teaching the steeples. It would be blind for more than a few years more to be discouraged about modern religion. The telephone, the wireless telegraph, the X-rays, and all the other great believers are singing up around it. The very railroads are surrounding it and taking care of it. A few years more and the steeples will stop hesitating and tottering in the sight of all the people. They will no longer stand in fear before what the crowds of chimneys and railways and the miles of smokestacks sweeping past are saying to the people.

They will listen to what the smokestacks are saying to the people.

They will say it better.

In the meantime they are not listening.

Religion and art at the present moment, both blindfolded and both with their ears stopped, are being swept to the same irrevocable issue. By all poets and prophets the same danger signal shall be seen spreading before them both jogging along their old highways. It is the arm that reaches across the age.

RAILROAD CROSSING

LOOK OUT FOR THE ENGINE!

PART II.
THE LANGUAGE OF THE MACHINES.

I

AS GOOD AS OURS

One is always hearing it said that if a thing is to be called poetic it must have great ideas in it, and must successfully express them. The idea that there is poetry in machinery, has to meet the objection that, while a machine may have great ideas in it, "it does not look it." The average machine not only fails to express the idea that it stands for, but it generally expresses something else. The language of the average machine, when one considers what it is for, what it is actually doing, is not merely irrelevant or feeble. It is often absurd. It is a rare machine which, when one looks for poetry in it, does not make itself ridiculous.

The only answer that can be made to this objection is that a steam-engine (when one thinks of it) really expresses itself as well as the rest of us. All language is irrelevant, feeble, and absurd. We live in an organically inexpressible world. The language of everything in it is absurd. Judged merely by its outer signs, the universe over our heads—with its cunning little stars in it—is the height of absurdity, as a self-expression. The sky laughs at us. We know it when we look in a telescope. Time and space are God's jokes. Looked at strictly in its outer language, the whole visible world is a joke. To suppose that God has ever expressed Himself to us in it, or to suppose that He could express Himself in it, or that any one can express anything in it, is not to see the point of the joke.

We cannot even express ourselves to one another. The language of everything we use or touch is absurd. Nearly all of the tools we do our living with—even the things that human beings amuse themselves with—are inexpressive and foolish-looking. Golf and tennis and football have all been accused in turn, by people who do not know them from the inside, of being meaningless. A golf-stick does not convey anything to the uninitiated, but the bare sight of a golf-stick lying on a seat is a feeling to the one to whom it belongs, a play of sense and spirit to him, a subtle thrill in his arms. The same is true of a new fiery-red baby, which, considering the fuss that is made about it, to a comparative outsider like a small boy, has always been from the beginning of the world a ridiculous and inadequate object. A man could not possibly conceive, even if he gave all his time to it, of a more futile, reckless, hapless expression of or pointer to an immortal soul than a week-old baby wailing at time and space. The idea of a baby may be all right, but in its outer form, at first, at least, a baby is a failure, and always has been. The same is true of our other musical instruments. A horn caricatures music. A flute is a man rubbing a black stick with his lips. A trombone player is a monster. We listen solemnly to the violin—the voice of an archangel with a board tucked under his chin—and to Girardi's 'cello—a whole human race laughing and crying and singing to us between a boy's legs. The eye-language of the violin has to be interpreted, and only people who are cultivated enough to suppress whole parts of themselves (rather useful and important parts elsewhere) can enjoy a great opera—a huge conspiracy of symbolism, every visible thing in it standing for something that can not be seen, beckoning at something that cannot be heard. Nothing could possibly be more grotesque, looked at from the outside or by a tourist from another planet or another religion, than the celebration of the Lord's Supper in a Protestant church. All things have their outer senses, and these outer senses have to be learned one at a time by being flashed through with inner ones. Except to people who have tried it, nothing could be more grotesque than kissing, as a form of human expression. A reception—a roomful of people shouting at each other three inches away— is comical enough. So is handshaking. Looked at from the outside, what could be more unimpressive than the spectacle of the greatest dignitary of the United States put in a vise in his own house for three hours, having his hand squeezed by long rows of people? And, taken as a whole, scurrying about in its din, what could possibly be more grotesque than a great city—a city looked at from almost any adequate, respectable place for an immortal soul to look from—a star, for instance, or a beautiful life?

Whether he is looked at by ants or by angels, every outer token that pertains to man is absurd and unfinished until some inner thing is put with it. Man himself is futile and comic-looking (to the other animals), rushing empty about space. New York is a spectacle for a squirrel to laugh at, and, from the point of view of a mouse, a man is a mere, stupid, sitting-down, skull-living, desk-infesting animal.

All these things being true of expression—both the expression of men and of God—the fact that machines which have poetry in them do not express it very well does not trouble me much. I do not forget the look of the first ocean-engine I ever saw—four or five stories of it; nor do I forget the look of the ocean-engine's engineer as in its mighty heart-beat he stood with his strange, happy, helpless "Twelve thousand horse-power, sir!" upon his lips.

That first night with my first engineer still follows me. The time seems always coming back to me again when he brought me up from his whirl of wheels in the hold to the deck of stars, and left me—my new wonder all stumbling through me—alone with them and with my thoughts.

The engines breathe.

No sound but cinders on the sails

And the ghostly heave,

The voice the wind makes in the mast—

And dainty gales

And fluffs of mist and smoking stars

Floating past—

From night-lit funnels.

In the wild of the heart of God I stand.

Time and Space

Wheel past my face.

Forever. Everywhere.

I alone.

Beyond the Here and There

Now and Then

Of men,

Winds from the unknown

Round me blow

Blow to the unknown again.

Out in its solitude I hear the prow

Beyond the silence-crowded decks

Laughing and shouting

At Night,

Lashing the heads and necks

Of the lifted seas,

That in their flight

Urge onward

And rise and sweep and leap and sink

To the very brink

Of Heaven.

Timber and steel and smoke

And Sleep

Thousand-souled

A quiver,

A deadened thunder,

A vague and countless creep

Through the hold,

The weird and dusky chariot lunges on

Through Fate.

From the lookout watch of my soul's eyes

Above the houses of the deep

Their shadowy haunches fall and rise

—O'er the glimmer-gabled roofs

The flying of their hoofs,

Through the wonder and the dark

Where skies and waters meet

The shimmer of manes and knees

Dust of seas...

The sound of breathing, urge, confusion

And the beat, the starlight beat

Soft and far and stealthy-fleet

Of the dim unnumbered trampling of their feet.

ON BEING BUSY AND STILL

One of the hardest things about being an inventor is that the machines (excepting the poorer ones) never show off. The first time that the phonograph (whose talking had been rumored of many months) was allowed to talk in public, it talked to an audience in Metuchen, New Jersey, and, much to Mr. Edison's dismay, everybody laughed. Instead of being impressed with the real idea of the phonograph—being impressed because it could talk at all—people were impressed because it talked through its nose.

The more modern a machine is, when a man stands before it and seeks to know it,—the more it expects of the man, the more it appeals to his imagination and his soul,—the less it is willing to appeal to the outside of him. If he will not look with his whole being at a twin-screw steamer, he will not see it. Its poetry is under water. This is one of the chief characteristics of the modern world, that its poetry is under water. The old sidewheel steamer floundering around in the big seas, pounding the air and water both with her huge, showy paddles, is not so poetic-looking as the sailboat, and the poetry in the sailboat is not so obvious, so plainly on top, as in a gondola.

People who do not admit poetry in machinery in general admit that there is poetry in a Dutch windmill, because the poetry is in sight. A Dutch windmill flourishes. The American windmill, being improved so much that it does not flourish, is supposed not to have poetry in it at all. The same general principle holds good with every machine that has been invented. The more the poet—that is, the inventor—works on it, the less the poetry in it shows. Progress in a modern machine, if one watches it in its various stages, always consists in making a machine stop posing and get down to work. The earlier locomotive, puffing helplessly along with a few cars on its crooked rails, was much more fire-breathing, dragon-like and picturesque than the present one, and the locomotive that came next, while very different, was more impressive than the present one. Every one remembers it,—the important-looking, bell-headed, woodpile-eating locomotive of thirty years ago, with its noisy steam-blowing habits and its ceaseless water-drinking habits, with its grim, spreading cowcatcher and its huge plug-hat—who does not remember it—fussing up and down stations, ringing its bell forever and whistling at everything in sight? It was impossible to travel on a train at all thirty years ago without always thinking of the locomotive. It shoved itself at people. It was always doing things—now at one end of the train and now at the other, ringing its bell down the track, blowing in at the windows, it fumed and spread enough in hauling three cars from Boston to Concord to get to Chicago and back. It was the poetic, old-fashioned way that engines were made. One takes a train from New York to San Francisco now, and scarcely knows there is an engine on it. All he knows is that he is going, and sometimes the going is so good he hardly knows that.

The modern engines, the short-necked, pin-headed, large-limbed, silent ones, plunging with smooth and splendid leaps down their aisles of space— engines without any faces, blind, grim, conquering, lifting the world—are more poetic to some of us than the old engines were, for the very reason that they are not so poetic-looking. They are less showy, more furtive, suggestive, modern and perfect.

In proportion as a machine is modern it hides its face. It refuses to look as poetic as it is; and if it makes a sound, it is almost always a sound that is too small for it, or one that belongs to some one else. The trolley-wire, lifting a whole city home to supper, is a giant with a falsetto voice. The large-sounding, the poetic-sounding, is not characteristic of the modern spirit. In so far as it exists at all in the modern age, either in its machinery or its poetry, it exists because it is accidental or left over. There was a deep bass steamer on the Mississippi once, with a very small head of steam, which any one would have admitted had poetry in it—old-fashioned poetry. Every time it whistled it stopped.

III

ON NOT SHOWING OFF

It is not true to say that the modern man does not care for poetry. He does not care for poetry that bears on—or for eloquent poetry. He cares for poetry in a new sense. In the old sense he does not care for eloquence in anything. The lawyer on the floor of Congress who seeks to win votes by a show of eloquence is turned down. Votes are facts, and if the votes are to be won, facts must be arranged to do it. The doctor who stands best with the typical modern patient is not the most agreeable, sociable, jogging-about man a town contains, like the doctor of the days gone by. He talks less. He even prescribes less, and the reason that it is hard to be a modern minister (already cut down from two hours and a half to twenty or thirty minutes) is that one has to practise more than one can preach.

To be modern is to be suggestive and symbolic, to stand for more than one says or looks—the little girl with her loom clothing twelve hundred people. People like it. They are used to it. All life around them is filled with it. The old-fashioned prayer-meeting is dying out in the modern church because it is a mere specialty in modern life. The prayer-meeting recognizes but one way of praying, and people who have a gift for praying that way go, but the majority of people—people who have discovered that there are a thousand other ways of praying, and who like them better—stay away.

When the telegraph machine was first thought of, the words all showed on the outside. When it was improved it became inner and subtle. The messages were read by sound. Everything we have which improves at all improves in the same way. The exterior conception of righteousness of a hundred years ago—namely, that a man must do right because it is his duty—is displaced by the modern one, the morally thorough one—namely, that a man must do right because he likes it—do it from the inside. The more improved righteousness is, the less it shows on the outside. The more modern righteousness is, the more it looks like selfishness, the better the modern world likes it, and the more it counts.

On the whole, it is against a thing rather than in its favor, in the twentieth century, that it looks large. Time was when if it had not been known as a matter of fact that Galileo discovered heaven with a glass three feet long, men would have said that it would hardly do to discover heaven with anything less than six hundred feet long. To the ancients, Galileo's instrument, even if it had been practical, would not have been poetic or fitting. To the moderns, however, the fact that Galileo's star-tool was three feet long, that he carried a new heaven about with him in his hands, was half the poetry and wonder of it. Yet it was not so poetic-looking as the six-hundred-foot telescope invented later, which never worked.

Nothing could be more impressive than the original substantial R—— typewriter. One felt, every time he touched a letter, as if he must have said a sentence. It was like saying things with pile-drivers. The machine obtruded itself at every point. It flourished its means and ends. It was a gesticulating machine. One commenced every new line with his foot.

The same general principle may be seen running alike through machinery and through life. The history of man is traced in water-wheels. The overshot wheel belonged to a period when everything else—religion, literature, and art—was overshot. When, as time passed on, common men began to think, began to think under a little, the Reformation came in—and the undershot wheel, as a matter of course. There is no denying that the overshot wheel is more poetic-looking—it does its work with twelve quarts of water at a time and shows every quart—but it soon develops into the undershot wheel, which shows only the drippings of the water, and the undershot wheel develops into the turbine wheel, which keeps everything out of sight—except its work. The water in the six turbine wheels at Niagara has sixty thousand horses in it, but it is not nearly as impressive and poetic-looking as six turbine wheels' worth of water would be—wasted and going over the Falls.

The main fact about the modern man as regards poetry is, that he prefers poetry that has this reserved turbine-wheel trait in it. It is because most of the poetry the modern man gets a chance to see to-day is merely going over the Falls that poetry is not supposed to appeal to the modern man. He supposes so himself. He supposes that a dynamo (forty street-cars on forty streets, flying through the dark) is not poetic, but its whir holds him, sense and spirit, spellbound, more than any poetry that is being written. The things that are hidden—the things that are spiritual and wondering—are the ones that appeal to him. The idle, foolish look of a magnet fascinates him. He gropes in his own body silently, harmlessly with the X-ray, and watches with awe the beating of his heart. He glories in inner essences, both in his life and in his art. He is the disciple of the X-ray, the defier of appearances. Why should a man who has seen the inside of matter care about appearances, either in little things or great? Or why argue about the man, or argue about the man's God, or quibble with words? Perhaps he is matter. Perhaps he is spirit. If he is spirit, he is matter-loving spirit, and if he is matter, he is spirit-loving matter. Every time he touches a spiritual thing, he makes it (as God makes mountains out of sunlight) a material thing. Every time he touches a material thing, in proportion as he touches it mightily he brings out inner light in it. He spiritualizes it. He abandons the glistening brass knocker—pleasing symbol to the outer sense—for a tiny knob on his porch door and a far-away tinkle in his kitchen. The brass knocker does not appeal to the spirit enough for the modern man, nor to the imagination. He wants an inner world to draw on to ring a door-bell with. He loves to wake the unseen. He will not even ring a door-bell if he can help it. He likes it better, by touching a button, to have a door-bell rung for him by a couple of metals down in his cellar chewing each other. He likes to reach down twelve flights of stairs with a thrill on a wire and open his front door. He may be seen riding in three stories along his streets, but he takes his engines all off the tracks and crowds them into one engine and puts it out of sight. The more a thing is out of the sight of his eyes the more his soul sees it and glories in it. His fireplace is underground. Hidden water spouts over his head and pours beneath his feet through his house. Hidden light creeps through the dark in it. The more might, the more subtlety. He hauls the whole human race around the crust of the earth with a vapor made out of a solid. He stops solids—sixty miles an hour—with invisible air. He photographs the tone of his voice on a platinum plate. His voice reaches across death with the platinum plate. He is heard of the unborn. If he speaks in either one of his worlds he takes two worlds to speak with. He will not be shut in with one. If he lives in either he wraps the other about him. He makes men walk on air. He drills out rocks with a cloud and he breaks open mountains with gas. The more perfect he makes his machines the more spiritual they are, the more their power hides itself. The more the machines of the man loom in human life the more they reach down into silence, and into darkness. Their foundations are infinity. The infinity which is the man's infinity is their infinity. The machines grasp all space for him. They lean out on ether. They are the man's machines. The man has made them and the man worships with them. From the first breath of flame, burning out the secret of the Dust to the last shadow of the dust—the breathless, soundless shadow of the dust, which he calls electricity—the man worships the invisible, the intangible. Electricity is his prophet. It sums him up. It sums up his modern world and the religion and the arts of his modern world. Out of all the machines that he has made the electric machine is the most modern because it is the most spiritual. The empty and futile look of a trolley wire does not trouble the modern man. It is his instinctive expression of himself. All the habits of electricity are his habits. Electricity has the modern man's temperament—the passion of being invisible and irresistible. The electric machine fills him with brotherhood and delight. It is the first of the machines that he can not help seeing is like himself. It is the symbol of the man's highest self. His own soul beckons to him out of it.

And the more electricity grows the more like the man it grows, the more spirit-like it is. The telegraph wire around the globe is melted into the wireless telegraph. The words of his spirit break away from the dust. They envelop the earth like ether, and Human Speech, at last, unconquerable, immeasurable, subtle as the light of stars,—fights its way to God.

The man no longer gropes in the dull helpless ground or through the froth of heaven for the spirit. Having drawn to him the X-ray, which makes spirit out of dust, and the wireless telegraph, which makes earth out of air, he delves into the deepest sea as a cloud. He strides heaven. He has touched the hem of the garment at last of ELECTRICITY—the archangel of matter.

IV

ON MAKING PEOPLE PROUD OF THE WORLD

Religion consists in being proud of the Creator. Poetry is largely the same feeling—a kind of personal joy one takes in the way the world is made and is being made every morning. The true lover of nature is touched with a kind of cosmic family pride every time he looks up from his work—sees the night and morning, still and splendid, hanging over him. Probably if there were another universe than this one, to go and visit in, or if there were an extra Creator we could go to—some of us—and boast about the one we have, it would afford infinite relief among many classes of people—especially poets.

The most common sign that poetry, real poetry, exists in the modern human heart is the pride that people are taking in the world. The typical modern man, whatever may be said or not said of his religion, of his attitude toward the maker of the world, has regular and almost daily habits of being proud of the world.

In the twentieth century the best way for a man to worship God is going to be to realize his own nature, to recognize what he is for, and be a god, too. We believe to-day that the best recognition of God consists in recognizing the fact that he is not a mere God who does divine things himself, but a God who can make others do them.

Looked at from the point of view of a mere God who does divine things himself, an earthquake, for instance, may be called a rather feeble affair, a slight jar to a ball going —— miles an hour—a Creator could do little less, if He gave a bare thought to it—but when I waked a few mornings ago and felt myself swinging in my own house as if it were a hammock, and was told that some men down in Hazardville, Connecticut, had managed to shake the planet like that, with some gunpowder they had made, I felt a new respect for Messrs. —— and Co. I was proud of man, my brother. Does he not shake loose the Force of Gravity—make the very hand of God to tremble? To his thoughts the very hills, with their hearts of stone, make soft responses—when he thinks them.

The Corliss engine of Machinery Hall in '76, under its sky of iron and glass, is remembered by many people the day they saw it first as one of the great experiences of life. Like some vast, Titanic spirit, soul of a thousand, thousand wheels, it stood to some of us, in its mighty silence there, and wrought miracles. To one twelve-year-old boy, at least, the thought of the hour he spent with that engine first is a thought he sings and prays with to this day. His lips trembled before it. He sought to hide himself in its presence. Why had no one ever taught him anything before? As he looks back through his life there is one experience that stands out by itself in all those boyhood years—the choking in his throat—the strange grip upon him—upon his body and upon his soul—as of some awful unseen Hand reaching down Space to him, drawing him up to Its might. He was like a dazed child being held up before It—held up to an infinite fact, that he might look at it again and again.

The first conception of what the life of man was like, of what it might be like, came to at least one immortal soul not from lips that he loved, or from a face behind a pulpit, or a voice behind a desk, but from a machine. To this day that Corliss engine is the engine of dreams, the appeal to destiny, to the imagination and to the soul. It rebuilds the universe. It is the opportunity of beauty throughout life, the symbol of freedom, the freedom of men, and of the unity of nations, and of the worship of God. In silence—like the soft far running of the sky—it wrought upon him there; like some heroic human spirit, its finger on a thousand wheels, through miles of aisles, and crowds of gazers, it wrought. The beat and rhythm of it was as the beat and rhythm of the heart of man mastering matter, of the clay conquering God.

Like some wonder-crowded chorus its voices surrounded me. It was the first hearing of the psalm of life. The hum and murmur of it was like the spell of ages upon me; and the vision that floated in it—nay, the vision that was builded in it—was the vision of the age to be: the vision of Man, My Brother, after the singsong and dance and drone of his sad four thousand years, lifting himself to the stature of his soul at last, lifting himself with the sun, and with the rain, and with the wind, and the heat and the light, into comradeship with Creation morning, and into something (in our far-off, wistful fashion) of the might and gentleness of God.

There seem to be two ways to worship Him. One way is to gaze upon the great Machine that He has made, to watch it running softly above us all, moonlight and starlight, and winter and summer, rain and snowflakes, and growing things. Another way is to worship Him not only because He has made the vast and still machine of creation, in the beating of whose days and nights we live our lives, but because He has made a Machine that can make machines—because out of the dust of the earth He has made a Machine that shall take more of the dust of the earth, and of the vapor of heaven, crowd it into steel and iron and say, "Go ye now, depths of the earth—heights of heaven—serve ye me. I, too, am God. Stones and mists, winds and waters and thunder—the spirit that is in thee is my spirit. I also—even I also—am God!"

V

A MODEST UNIVERSE

I have heard it objected that a machine does not take hold of a man with its great ideas while he stands and watches it. It does not make him feel its great ideas. And therefore it is denied that it is poetic.

The impressiveness of the bare spiritual facts of machinery is not denied. What seems to be lacking in the machines from the artistic point of view at present is a mere knack of making the faces plain and literal-looking. Grasshoppers would be more appreciated by more people if they were made with microscopes on,—either the grasshoppers or the people.

If the mere machinery of a grasshopper's hop could be made plain and large enough, there is not a man living who would not be impressed by it. If grasshoppers were made (as they might quite as easily have been) 640 feet high, the huge beams of their legs above their bodies towering like cranes against the horizon, the sublimity of a grasshopper's machinery—the huge levers of it, his hops across valleys from mountain to mountain, shadowing fields and villages—would have been one of the impressive features of human life. Everybody would be willing to admit of the mere machinery of a grasshopper, (if there were several acres of it) that there was creative sublimity in it. They would admit that the bare idea of having such a stately piece of machinery in a world at all, slipping softly around on it, was an idea with creative sublimity in it; and yet these same people because the sublimity, instead of being spread over several acres, is crowded into an inch and a quarter, are not impressed by it.

But it is objected, it is not merely a matter of spiritual size. There is something more than plainness lacking in the symbolism of machinery. "The symbolism of machinery is lacking in fitness. It is not poetic." "A thing can only be said to be poetic in proportion as its form expresses its nature." Mechanical inventions may stand for impressive facts, but such inventions, no matter how impressive the facts may be, cannot be called poetic unless their form expresses those facts. A horse plunging and champing his bits on the eve of battle, for instance, is impressive to a man, and a pill-box full of dynamite, with a spark creeping toward it, is not.

That depends partly on the man and partly on the spark. A man may not be impressed by a pill-box full of dynamite and a spark creeping toward it, the first time he sees it, but the second time he sees it, if he has time, he is impressed enough. He does not stand and criticise the lack of expression in pill-boxes, nor wait to remember the day when he all but lost his life because

A pill-box by the river's brim

A simple pill-box was to him

And nothing more.

Wordsworth in these memorable lines has summed up and brought to an issue the whole matter of poetry in machinery. Everything has its language, and the power of feeling what a thing means, by the way it looks, is a matter of experience—of learning the language. The language is there. The fact that the language of the machine is a new language, and a strangely subtle one, does not prove that it is not a language, that its symbolism is not good, and that there is not poetry in machinery.

The inventor need not be troubled because in making his machine it does not seem to express. It is written that neither you nor I, comrade nor God, nor any man, nor any man's machine, nor God's machine, in this world shall express or be expressed. If it is the meaning of life to us to be expressed in it, to be all-expressed, we are indeed sorry, dumb, plaintive creatures dotting a star awhile, creeping about on it, warmed by a heater ninety-five million miles away. The machine of the universe itself, does not express its Inventor. It does not even express the men who are under it. The ninety-five millionth mile waits on us silently, at the doorways of our souls night and day, and we wait on IT. Is it not THERE? Is it not HERE—this ninety-five millionth mile? It is ours. It runs in our veins. Why should Man—a being who can live forever in a day, who is born of a boundless birth, who takes for his fireside the immeasurable—express or expect to be expressed? What we would like to be—even what we are—who can say? Our music is an apostrophe to dumbness. The Pantomime above us rolls softly, resistlessly on, over the pantomime within us. We and our machines, both, hewing away on the infinite, beckon and are still.

I am not troubled because the machines do not seem to express themselves. I do not know that they can express themselves. I know that when the day is over, and strength is spent, and my soul looks out upon the great plain— upon the soft, night-blooming cities, with their huge machines striving in sleep, might lifts itself out upon me. I rest.

I know that when I stand before a foundry hammering out the floors of the world, clashing its awful cymbals against the night, I lift my soul to it, and in some way I know not how—while it sings to me I grow strong and glad.

PART THREE
THE MACHINES AS POETS

I

PLATO AND THE GENERAL ELECTRIC WORKS

I have an old friend who lives just around the corner from one of the main lines of travel in New England, and whenever I am passing near by and the railroads let me, I drop in on him awhile and quarrel about art. It's a good old-fashioned comfortable, disorderly conversation we have generally, the kind people used to have more than they do now—sketchy and not too wise—the kind that makes one think of things one wishes one had said, afterward.

We always drift a little at first, as if of course we could talk about other things if we wanted to, but we both know, and know every time, that in a few minutes we shall be deep in a discussion of the Things That Are Beautiful and the Things That Are Not.

Brim thinks that I have picked out more things to be beautiful than I have a right to, or than any man has, and he is trying to put a stop to it. He thinks that there are enough beautiful things in this world that have been beautiful a long while, without having people—well, people like me, for instance, poking blindly around among all these modern brand-new things hoping that in spite of appearances there is something one can do with them that will make them beautiful enough to go with the rest. I'm afraid Brim gets a little personal in talking with me at times and I might as well say that, while disagreeing in a conversation with Brim does not lead to calling names it does seem to lead logically to one's going away, and trying to find afterwards, some thing that is the matter with him.

"The trouble with you, my dear Brim, is," I say (on paper, afterwards, as the train speeds away), "that you have a false-classic or Stucco-Greek mind. The Greeks, the real Greeks, would have liked all these things—trolley cars, cables, locomotives,—seen the beautiful in them, if they had to do their living with them every day, the way we do. You would say you were more Greek than I am, but when one thinks of it, you are just going around liking the things the Greeks liked 3000 years ago, and I am around liking the things a Greek would like now, that is, as well as I can. I don't flatter myself I begin to enjoy the wireless telegraph to-day the way Plato would if he had the chance, and Alcibiades in an automobile would get a great deal more out of it, I suspect, than anyone I have seen in one, so far; and I suspect that if Socrates could take Bliss Carman and, say, William Watson around with him on a tour of the General Electric Works in Schenectady they wouldn't either of them write sonnets about anything else for the rest of their natural lives."

I can only speak for one and I do not begin to see the poetry in the machines that a Greek would see, as yet.

But I have seen enough.

I have seen engineers go by, pounding on this planet, making it small enough, welding the nations together before my eyes.

I have seen inventors, still men by lamps at midnight with a whirl of visions, with a whirl of thoughts, putting in new drivewheels on the world.

I have seen (in Schenectady,) all those men—the five thousand of them— the grime on their faces and the great caldrons of melted railroad swinging above their heads. I have stood and watched them there with lightning and with flame hammering out the wills of cities, putting in the underpinnings of nations, and it seemed to me me that Bliss Carman and William Watson would not be ashamed of them ... brother-artists every one ... in the glory ... in the dark ... Vulcan-Tennysons, blacksmiths to a planet, with dredges, skyscrapers, steam shovels and wireless telegraphs, hewing away on the heavens and the earth.

II

HEWING AWAY ON THE HEAVENS AND THE EARTH

The poetry of machinery to-day is a mere matter of fact—a part of the daily wonder of life to countless silent people. The next thing the world wants to know about machinery is not that there is poetry in it, but that the poetry which the common people have already found there, has a right to be there. We have the fact. It is the theory to put with the fact which concerns us next and which really troubles us most. There are very few of us, on the whole, who can take any solid comfort in a fact—no matter what it is—until we have a theory to approve of it with. Its merely being a fact does not seem to make very much difference.

1. Machinery has poetry in it because it is an expression of the soul.

2. It expresses the soul (1) of the individual man who creates the machine—the inventor, and (2) the man who lives with the machine the engineer.

3. It expresses God, if only that He is a God who can make men who can thus express their souls. Machinery is an act of worship in the least sense if not in the greatest. If a man who can make machines like this is not clever enough with all his powers to find a God, and to worship a God, he can worship himself. It is because the poetry of machinery is the kind of poetry that does immeasurable things instead of immeasurably singing about them that it has been quite generally taken for granted that it is not poetry at all. The world has learned more of the purely poetic idea of freedom from a few dumb, prosaic machines that have not been able to say anything beautiful about it than from the poets of twenty centuries. The machine frees a hundred thousand men and smokes. The poet writes a thousand lines on freedom and has his bust in Westminster Abbey. The blacks in America were freed by Abraham Lincoln and the cotton gin. The real argument for unity—the argument against secession—was the locomotive. No one can fight the locomotive very long. It makes the world over into one world whether it wants to be one world or not. China is being conquered by steamships. It cannot be said that the idea of unity is a new one. Seers and poets have made poetry out of it for two thousand years. Machinery is making the poetry mean something. Every new invention in matter that comes to us is a spiritual masterpiece. It is crowded with ideas. The Bessemer process has more political philosophy in it than was ever dreamed of in Shelley's poetry, and it would not be hard to show that the invention of the sewing machine was one of the most literary and artistic as well as one of the most religious events of the nineteenth century. The loom is the most beautiful thought that any one has ever had about Woman, and the printing press is more wonderful than anything that has ever been said on it.

"This is all very true," interrupts the Logical Person, "about printing presses and looms and everything else—one could go on forever—but it does not prove anything. It may be true that the loom has made twenty readers for Robert Browning's poetry where Browning would have made but one, but it does not follow that because the loom has freed women for beauty that the loom is beautiful, or that it is a fit theme for poetry." "Besides"—breaks in the Minor Poet—"there is a difference between a thing's being full of big ideas and its being beautiful. A foundry is powerful and interesting, but is it beautiful the way an electric fountain is beautiful or a sonnet or a doily?"

This brings to a point the whole question as to where the definition of beauty—the boundary line of beauty—shall be placed. A thing's being considered beautiful is largely a matter of size. The question "Is a thing beautiful?" resolves itself into "How large has a beautiful thing a right to be?" A man's theory of beauty depends, in a universe like this, upon how much of the universe he will let into it. If he is afraid of the universe if he only lets his thoughts and passions live in a very little of it, he is apt to assume that if a beautiful thing rises into the sublime and immeasurable—suggests boundless ideas—the beauty is blurred out of it. It is something—there is no denying that it is something—but, whatever it is or is not, it is not beauty. Nearly everything in our modern life is getting too big to be beautiful. Our poets are dumb because they see more poetry than their theories have room for. The fundamental idea of the poetry of machinery is infinity. Our theories of poetry were made—most of them—before infinity was discovered.

Infinity itself is old, and the idea that infinity exists—a kind of huge, empty rim around human life—is not a new idea to us, but the idea that this same infinity has or can have anything to do with us or with our arts, or our theories of art, or that we have anything to do with IT, is an essentially modern discovery. The actual experience of infinity—that is, the experience of being infinite (comparatively speaking)—as in the use of machinery, is a still more modern discovery. There is no better way perhaps, of saying what modern machinery really is, than to say that it is a recent invention for being infinite.

The machines of the world are all practically engaged in manufacturing the same thing. They are all time-and-space-machines. They knit time and space. Hundreds of thousands of things may be put in machines this very day, for us, before night falls, but only eternity and infinity shall be turned out. Sometimes it is called one and sometimes the other. If a man is going to be infinite or eternal it makes little difference which. It is merely a matter of form whether one is everywhere a few years, or anywhere forever. A sewing machine is as much a means of communication as a printing press or a locomotive. The locomotive takes a woman around the world. The sewing machine gives her a new world where she is. At every point where a machine touches the life of a human being, it serves him with a new measure of infinity.

This would seem to be a poetic thing for a machine to do. Traditional poetry does not see any poetry in it, because, according to our traditions poetry has fixed boundary lines, is an old, established institution in human life, and infinity is not.

No one has wanted to be infinite before. Poetry in the ancient world was largely engaged in protecting people from the Infinite. They were afraid of it. They could not help feeling that the Infinite was over them. Worship consisted in propitiating it, poetry in helping people to forget it. With the exception of Job, the Hebrews almost invariably employed a poet—when they could get one—as a kind of transfigured policeman—to keep the sky off. It was what was expected of poets.

The Greeks did the same thing in a different way. The only difference was, that the Greeks, instead of employing their poets to keep the sky off, employed them to make it as much like the earth as possible—a kind of raised platform which was less dreadful and more familiar and homelike and answered the same general purpose. In other words, the sky became beautiful to the Greek when he had made it small enough. Making it small enough was the only way a Greek knew of making it beautiful.

Galileo knew another way. It is because Galileo knew another way—because he knew that the way to make the sky beautiful, was to make it large enough—that men are living in a new world. A new religion beats down through space to us. A new poetry lifts away the ceilings of our dreams. The old sky, with its little tent of stars, its film of flame and darkness burning over us, has floated to the past. The twentieth century—the home of the Infinite—arches over our human lives. The heaven is no longer, to the sons of men, a priests' wilderness, nor is it a poet's heaven—a paper, painted heaven, with little painted paper stars in it, to hide the wilderness.

It is a new heaven. Who, that has lived these latter years, that has seen it crashing and breaking through the old one, can deny that what is over us now is a new heaven? The infinite cave of it, scooped out at last over our little naked, foolish lives, our running-about philosophies, our religions, and our governments—it is the main fact about us. Arts and literatures—ants under a stone, thousands of years, blind with light, hither and thither, racing about, hiding themselves.

But not long for dreams. More than this. The new heaven is matched by a new earth. Men who see a new heaven make a new earth. In its cloud of steam, in a kind of splendid, silent stammer of praise and love, the new earth lifts itself to the new heaven, lifts up days out of nights to It, digs wells for winds under It, lights darkness with falling water, makes ice out of vapor, and heat out of cold, draws down Space with engines, makes years out of moments with machines. It is a new world and all the men that are born upon it are new widemoving, cloud and mountain-moving men. The habits of stars and waters, the huge habits of space and time, are the habits of the men.

The Infinite, at last, which in days gone by hung over us—the mere hiding place of Death, the awful living-room of God—is the neighborhood of human life.

Machinery has poetry in it because in expressing the soul it expresses the greatest idea that the soul of man can have, namely, the idea that the soul of man is infinite, or capable of being infinite.

Machinery has poetry in it also not merely because it is the symbol of infinite power in human life, or because it makes man think he is infinite, but because it is making him as infinite as he thinks he is. The infinity of man is no longer a thing that the poet takes—that he makes an idea out of—Machinery makes it a matter of fact.

III

THE GRUDGE AGAINST THE INFINITE

The main thing the nineteenth century has done in literature has been the gradual sorting out of poets into two classes—those who like the infinite, who have a fellow-feeling for it, and those who have not. It seems reasonable to say that the poets who have habits of infinity, of space-conquering (like our vast machines), who seek the suggestive and immeasurable in the things they see about them—poets who like infinity, will be the poets to whom we will have to look to reveal to us the characteristic and real poetry of this modern world. The other poets, it is to be feared, are not even liking the modern world, to say nothing of singing in it. They do not feel at home in it. The classic-walled poet seems to feel exposed in our world. It is too savagely large, too various and unspeakable and unfinished. He looks at the sky of it—the vast, unkempt, unbounded sky of it, to which it sings and lifts itself—with a strange, cold, hidden dread down in his heart. To him it is a mere vast, dizzy, dreary, troubled formlessness. Its literature—its art with its infinite life in it, is a blur of vagueness. He complains because mobs of images are allowed in it. It is full of huddled associations. When Carlyle appeared, the Stucco-Greek mind grudgingly admitted that he was 'effective.' A man who could use words as other men used things, who could put a pen down on paper in such a way as to lift men out from the boundaries of their lives and make them live in other lives and in other ages, who could lend them his own soul, had to have something said about him; something very good and so it was said, but he was not an "artist." From the same point of view and to the same people Browning was a mere great man (that is: a merely infinite man). He was a man who went about living and loving things, with a few blind words opening the eyes of the blind. It had to be admitted that Robert Browning could make men who had never looked at their brothers' faces dwell for days in their souls, but he was not a poet. Richard Wagner, too, seer, lover, singer, standing in the turmoil of his violins conquering a new heaven for us, had great conceptions and was a musical genius without the slightest doubt, but he was not an "artist." He never worked his conceptions out. His scores are gorged with mere suggestiveness. They are nothing if they are not played again and again. For twenty or thirty years Richard Wagner was outlawed because his music was infinitely unfinished (like the music of the spheres). People seemed to want him to write cosy, homelike music.

IV

SYMBOLISM IN MODERN ART

"So I drop downward from the wonderment

Of timelessness and space, in which were blent

The wind, the sunshine and the wanderings

Of all the planets—to the little things

That are my grass and flowers, and am content."

This prejudice against the infinite, or desire to avoid as much as possible all personal contact with it, betrays itself most commonly, perhaps, in people who have what might be called the domestic feeling, who consciously or unconsciously demand the domestic touch in a landscape before they are ready to call it beautiful. The typical American woman, unless she has unusual gifts or training, if she is left entirely to herself, prefers nice cuddlesome scenery. Even if her imagination has been somewhat cultivated and deepened, so that she feels that a place must be wild, or at least partly wild, in order to be beautiful, she still chooses nooks and ravines, as a rule, to be happy in—places roofed in with gentle, quiet wonder, fenced in with beauty on every side. She is not without her due respect and admiration for a mountain, but she does not want it to be too large, or too near the stars, if she has to live with it day and night; and if the truth were told—even at its best she finds a mountain distant, impersonal, uncompanionable. Unless she is born in it she does not see beauty in the wide plain. There is something in her being that makes her bashful before a whole sky; she wants a sunset she can snuggle up to. It is essentially the bird's taste in scenery. "Give me a nest, O Lord, under the wide heaven. Cover me from Thy glory." A bush or a tree with two or three other bushes or trees near by, and just enough sky to go with it—is it not enough?

The average man is like the average woman in this regard except that he is less so. The fact seems to be that the average human being (like the average poet), at least for everyday purposes, does not want any more of the world around him than he can use, or than he can put somewhere. If there is so much more of the world than one can use, or than anyone else can use, what is the possible object of living where one cannot help being reminded of it?

The same spiritual trait, a kind of gentle persistent grudge against the infinite, shows itself in the not uncommon prejudice against pine trees. There are a great many people who have a way of saying pleasant things about pine trees and who like to drive through them or look at them in the landscape or have them on other people's hills, but they would not plant a pine tree near their houses or live with pines singing over them and watching them, every day and night, for the world. The mood of the pine is such a vast, still, hypnotic, imperious mood that there are very few persons, no matter how dull or unsusceptible they may seem to be, who are not as much affected by a single pine, standing in a yard by a doorway, as they are by a whole skyful of weather. If they are down on the infinite—they do not want a whole treeful of it around on the premises. And the pine comes as near to being infinite as anything purely vegetable, in a world like this, could expect. It is the one tree of all others that profoundly suggests, every time the light falls upon it or the wind stirs through it, THE THINGS THAT MAN CANNOT TOUCH. Woven out of air and sunlight and its shred of dust, it always seems to stand the monument of the woods, to The Intangible, and The Invisible, to the spirituality of matter. Who shall find a tree that looks down upon the spirit of the pine? And who, who has ever looked upon the pines—who has seen them climbing the hills in crowds, drinking at the sun—has not felt that however we may take to them personally they are the Chosen People among the trees? To pass from the voice of them to the voice of the common leaves is to pass from the temple to the street. In the rest of the forest all the leaves seem to be full of one another's din—of rattle and chatter—heedless, happy chaos, but in the pines the voice of every pine-spill is as a chord in the voice of all the rest, and the whole solemn, measured chant of it floats to us as the voice of the sky itself. It is as if all the mystical, beautiful far-things that human spirits know had come from the paths of Space, and from the presence of God, to sing in the tree-trunks over our heads.

Now it seems to me that the supremacy of the pine in the imagination is not that it is more beautiful in itself than other trees, but that the beauty of the pine seems more symbolic than other beauty, and symbolic of more and of greater things. It is full of the sturdiness and strength of the ground, but it is of all trees the tree to see the sky with, and its voice is the voice of the horizons, the voice of the marriage of the heavens and the earth; and not only is there more of the sky in it, and more of the kingdom of the air and of the place of Sleep, but there is more of the fiber and odor from the solemn heart of the earth. No other tree can be mutilated like the pine by the hand of man and still keep a certain earthy, unearthly dignity and beauty about it and about all the place where it stands. A whole row of them, with their left arms cut off for passing wires, standing severe and stately, their bare trunks against heaven, cannot help being beautiful. The beauty is symbolic and infinite. It cannot be taken away. If the entire street-side of a row of common, ordinary middle-class trees were cut away there would be nothing to do with the maimed and helpless things but to cut them down—remove their misery from all men's sight. To lop away the half of a pine is only to see how beautiful the other half is. The other half has the infinite in it. However little of a pine is left it suggests everything there is. It points to the universe and beckons to the Night and the Day. The infinite still speaks in it. It is the optimist, the prophet of trees. In the sad lands it but grows more luxuriantly, and it is the spirit of the tropics in the snows. It is the touch of the infinite—of everywhere—wherever its shadow falls. I have heard the sound of a hammer in the street and it was the sound of a hammer. In the pine woods it was a hundred guns. As the cloud catches the great empty spaces of night out of heaven and makes them glorious the pine gathers all sound into itself—echoes it along the infinite.

The pine may be said to be the symbol of the beauty in machinery, because it is beautiful the way an electric light is beautiful, or an electric-lighted heaven. It has the two kinds of beauty that belong to life: finite beauty, in that its beauty can be seen in itself, and infinite beauty in that it makes itself the symbol, the center, of the beauty that cannot be seen, the beauty that dwells around it.

What is going to be called the typical power of the colossal art, myriad-nationed, undreamed of men before, now gathering in our modern life, is its symbolic power, its power of standing for more than itself.

Every great invention of modern mechanical art and modern fine art has held within it an extraordinary power of playing upon associations, of playing upon the spirits and essences of things until the outer senses are all gathered up, led on, and melted, as outer senses were meant to be melted, into inner ones. What is wrought before the eyes of a man at last by a great modern picture is not the picture that fronts him on the wall, but a picture behind the picture, painted with the flame of the heart on the eternal part of him. It is the business of a great modern work of art to bring a man face to face with the greatness from which it came. Millet's Angelus is a portrait of the infinite,—and a man and a woman. A picture with this feeling of the infinite painted in it—behind it—which produces this feeling of the infinite in other men by playing upon the infinite in their own lives, is a typical modern masterpiece.

The days when the infinite is not in our own lives we do not see it. If the infinite is in our own lives, and we do not like it there, we do not like it in a picture, or in the face of a man, or in a Corliss engine—a picture of the face of All-Man, mastering the earth—silent—lifted to heaven.

V

THE MACHINES AS ARTISTS

It is not necessary, in order to connect a railway train with the infinite, to see it steaming along a low sky and plunging into a huge white hill of cloud, as I did the other day. It is quite as infinite flying through granite in Hoosac Mountain. Most people who do not think there is poetry in a railway train are not satisfied with flying through granite as a trait of the infinite in a locomotive, and yet these same people, if a locomotive could be lifted bodily to where infinity is or is supposed to be (up in the sky somewhere)—if they could watch one night after night plowing through planets—would want a poem written about it at once.

A man who has a theory he does not see poetry in a locomotive, does not see it because theoretically he does not connect it with infinite things: the things that poetry is usually about. The idea that the infinite is not cooped up in heaven, that it can be geared and run on a track (and be all the more infinite for not running off the track), does not occur to him. The first thing he does when he is told to look for the infinite in the world is to stop and think a moment, where he is, and then look for it somewhere else.

It would seem to be the first idea of the infinite, in being infinite, not to be anywhere else. It could not be anywhere else if it tried; and if a locomotive is a real thing, a thing wrought in and out of the fiber of the earth and of the lives of men, the infinity and poetry in it are a matter of course. I like to think that it is merely a matter of seeing a locomotive as it is, of seeing it in enough of its actual relations as it is, to feel that it is beautiful; that the beauty, the order, the energy, and the restfulness of the whole universe are pulsing there through its wheels.

The times when we do not feel poetry in a locomotive are the times when we are not matter-of-fact enough. We do not see it in enough of its actual relations. Being matter-of-fact enough is all that makes anything poetic. Everything in the universe, seen as it is, is seen as the symbol, the infinitely connected, infinitely crowded symbol of everything else in the universe—the summing up of everything else—another whisper of God's.

Have I not seen the great Sun Itself, from out of its huge heaven, packed in a seed and blown about on a wind? I have seen the leaves of the trees drink all night from the stars, and when I have listened with my soul—thousands of years—I have heard The Night and The Day creeping softly through mountains. People called it geology.

It seems that if a man cannot be infinite by going to the infinite, he is going to be infinite where he is. He is carving it on the hills, tunneling it through the rocks of the earth, piling it up on the crust of it, with winds and waters and flame and steel he is writing it on all things—that he is infinite, that he will be infinite. The whole planet is his signature.

If what the modern man is trying to say in his modern age is his own infinity, it naturally follows that the only way a modern artist can be a great artist in a modern age is to say in that age that man is infinite, better than any one else is saying it.

The best way to express this infinity of man is to seek out the things in the life of the man which are the symbols of his infinity—which suggest his infinity the most—and then play on those symbols and let those symbols play on him. In other words the poet's program is something like this. The modern age means the infinity of man. Modern art means symbolism of man's infinity. The best symbol of the man's infinity the poet can find, in this world the man has made, is The Machine.

At least it seems so to me. I was looking out of my study window down the long track in the meadow the other morning and saw a smoke-cloud floating its train out of sight. A high wind was driving, and in long wavering folds the cloud lay down around the train. It was like a great Bird, close to the snow, forty miles an hour. For a moment it almost seemed that, instead of a train making a cloud, it was a cloud propelling a train—wing of a thousand tons. I have often before seen a broken fog towing a mountain, but never have I seen before, a train of cars with its engine, pulled by the steam escaping from its whistle. Of course the train out in my meadow, with its pillar of fire by night and of cloud by day hovering over it, is nothing new; neither is the tower of steam when it stands still of a winter morning building pyramids, nor the long, low cloud creeping back on the car-tops and scudding away in the light; but this mad and splendid Thing of Whiteness and Wind, riding out there in the morning, this ghost of a train—soul or look in the eyes of it, haunting it, gathering it all up, steel and thunder, into itself, catching it away into heaven—was one of the most magical and stirring sights I have seen for a long time. It came to me like a kind of Zeit-geist or passing of the spirit of the age.

When I looked again it was old 992 from the roundhouse escorting Number Eight to Springfield.

VI

THE MACHINES AS PHILOSOPHERS

If we could go into History as we go into a theatre, take our seats quietly, ring up the vast curtain on any generation we liked, and then could watch it—all those far off queer happy people living before our eyes, two or three hours—living with their new inventions and their last wonders all about them, they would not seem to us, probably to know why they were happy. They would merely be living along with their new things from day to day, in a kind of secret clumsy gladness.

Perhaps it is the same with us. The theories for poems have to be arranged after we have had them. The fundamental appeal of machinery seems to be to every man's personal everyday instinct and experience. We have, most of the time, neither words nor theories for it.

I do not think that our case must stand or fall with our theory. But there is something comfortable about a theory. A theory gives one permission to let ones self go—makes it seem more respectable to enjoy things. So I suggest something—the one I have used when I felt I had to have one. I have partitioned it off by itself and it can be skipped.

1. The substance of a beautiful thing is its Idea.

2. A beautiful thing is beautiful in proportion as its form reveals the nature of its substance, that is, conveys its idea.

3. Machinery is beautiful by reason of immeasurable ideas consummately expressed.

4. Machinery has poetry in it because the three immeasurable ideas expressed by machinery are the three immeasurable ideas of poetry and of the imagination and the soul—infinity and the two forms of infinity, the liberty and the unity of man.

5. These immeasurable ideas are consummately expressed by machinery because machinery expresses them in the only way that immeasurable ideas can ever be expressed: (1) by literally doing the immeasurable things, (2) by suggesting that it is doing them. To the man who is in the mood of looking at it with his whole being, the machine is beautiful because it is the mightiest and silentest symbol the world contains of the infinity of his own life, and of the liberty and unity of all men's lives, which slowly, out of the passion of history is now being wrought out before our eyes upon the face of the earth.

6. It is only from the point of view of a nightingale or a sonnet that the æsthetic form of a machine, if it is a good machine, can be criticised as unbeautiful. The less forms dealing with immeasurable ideas are finished

forms the more symbolic and speechless they are; the more they invoke the imagination and make it build out on God, and upon the Future, and upon Silence, the more artistic and beautiful and satisfying they are.

7. The first great artist a modern or machine age can have, will be the man who brings out for it the ideas behind its machines. These ideas—the ones the machines are daily playing over and about the lives of all of us—might be stated roughly as follows:

The idea of the incarnation—the god in the body of the man.

The idea of liberty—the soul's rescue from others.

The idea of unity—the soul's rescue from its mere self.

The idea of the Spirit—the Unseen and Intangible.

The idea of immortality.

The cosmic idea of God.

The practical idea of invoking great men.

The religious idea of love and comradeship.

And nearly every other idea that makes of itself a song or a prayer in the human spirit.

PART FOUR
IDEAS BEHIND THE MACHINES

I

THE IDEA OF INCARNATION

"I sought myself through earth and fire and seas,

And found it not—but many things beside;

Behemoth old, Leviathans that ride.

And protoplasm, and jellies of the tide.

Then wandering upward through the solid earth

With its dim sounds, potential rage and mirth,

I faced the dim Forefather of my birth,

And thus addressed Him: 'All of you that lie

Safe in the dust or ride along the sky—

Lo, these and these and these! But where am I?'"

The grasshopper may be called the poet of the insects. He has more hop for his size than any of the others. I am very fond of watching him—especially of watching those two enormous beams of his that loom up on either side of his body. They have always seemed to me one of the great marvels of mechanics. By knowing how to use them, he jumps forty times his own length. A man who could contrive to walk as well as any ordinary grasshopper does (and without half trying) could make two hundred and fifty feet at a step. There is no denying, of course, that the man does it, after his fashion, but he has to have a trolley to do it with. The man seems to prefer, as a rule, to use things outside to get what he wants inside. He has a way of making everything outside him serve him as if he had it on his own body— uses a whole universe every day without the trouble of always having to carry it around with him. He gets his will out of the ground and even out of the air. He lays hold of the universe and makes arms and legs out of it. If he wants at any time, for any reason, more body than he was made with, he has his soul reach out over or around the planet a little farther and draw it in for him.

The grasshopper, so far as I know, does not differ from the man in that he has a soul and body both, but his soul and body seem to be perfectly matched. He has his soul and body all on. It is probably the best (and the worst) that can be said of a grasshopper's soul, if he has one, that it is in his legs—that he really has his wits about him.

Looked at superficially, or from the point of view of the next hop, it can hardly be denied that the body the human soul has been fitted out with is a rather inferior affair. From the point of view of any respectable or ordinarily well-equipped animal the human body—the one accorded to the average human being in the great show of creation—almost looks sometimes as if God really must have made it as a kind of practical joke, in the presence of the other animals, on the rest of us. It looks as if He had suddenly decided at the very moment he was in the middle of making a body for a man, that out of all the animals man should be immortal—and had let it go at that. With the exception of the giraffe and perhaps the goose or camel and an extra fold or so in the hippopotamus, we are easily the strangest, the most unexplained-looking shape on the face of the earth. It is exceedingly unlikely that we are beautiful or impressive, at first at least, to any one but ourselves. Nearly all the things we do with our hands and feet, any animal on earth could tell us, are things we do not do as well as men did once, or as well as we ought to, or as well as we did when we were born. Our very babies are our superiors.

The only defence we are able to make when we are arraigned before the bar of creation, seems to be, that while some of the powers we have exhibited have been very obviously lost, we have gained some very fine new invisible ones. We are not so bad, we argue, after all,—our nerves, for instance,—the mentalized condition of our organs. And then, of course, there is the superior quality of our gray matter. When we find ourselves obliged to appeal in this pathetic way from the judgment of the brutes, or of those who, like them, insist on looking at us in the mere ordinary, observing, scientific, realistic fashion, we hint at our mysteriousness—a kind of mesh of mysticism there is in us. We tell them it cannot really be seen from the outside, how well our bodies work. We do not put it in so many words, but what we mean is, that we need to be cut up to be appreciated, or seen in the large, or in our more infinite relations. Our matter may not be very well arranged on us, perhaps, but we flatter ourselves that there is a superior unseen spiritual quality in it. It takes seers or surgeons to appreciate us—more of the same sort, etc. In the meantime (no man can deny the way things look) here we all are, with our queer, pale, little stretched-out legs and arms and things, floundering about on this earth, without even our clothes on, covering ourselves as best we can. And what could really be funnier than a human body living before The Great Sun under its frame of wood and glass, all winter and all summer … strange and bleached-looking, like celery, grown almost always under cloth, kept in the kind of cellar of cotton or wool it likes for itself, moving about or being moved about, the way it is, in thousands of queer, dependent, helpless-looking ways? The earth, we can well believe, as we go up and down in it is full of soft laughter at us. One cannot so much as go in swimming without feeling the fishes peeking around the rocks, getting their fun out of us in some still, underworld sort of way. We cannot help—a great many of us—feeling, in a subtle way, strange and embarrassed in the woods. Most of us, it is true, manage to keep up a look of being fairly at home on the planet by huddling up and living in cities. By dint of staying carefully away from the other animals, keeping pretty much by ourselves, and whistling a good deal and making a great deal of noise, called civilization, we keep each other in countenance after a fashion, but we are really the guys of the animal world, and when we stop to think of it and face the facts and see ourselves as the others see us, we cannot help acknowledging it. I, for one, rather like to, and have it done with.

It is getting to be one of my regular pleasures now, as I go up and down the world,—looking upon the man's body,—the little funny one that he thinks he has, and then stretching my soul and looking upon the one that he really has. When one considers what a man actually does, where he really lives, one sees very plainly that all that he has been allowed is a mere suggestion or hint of a body, a sort of central nerve or ganglion for his real self. A seed or spore of infinity, blown down on a star—held there by the grip, apparently, of Nothing—a human body is pathetic enough, looked at in itself. There is something indescribably helpless and wistful and reaching out and incomplete about it—a body made to pray with, perhaps, one might say, but not for action. All that it really comes to or is for, apparently, is a kind of light there is in it.

But the sea is its footpath. The light that is in it is the same light that reaches down to the central fires of the earth. It flames upon heaven. Helpless and unfinished-looking as it is, when I look upon it, I have seen the animals slinking to their holes before it, and worshipping, or following the light that is in it. The great waters and the great lights flock to it—this beckoning and a prayer for a body, which the man has.

I go into the printing room of a great newspaper. In a single flash of black and white the press flings down the world for him—birth, death, disgrace, honor and war and farce and love and death, sea and hills, and the days on the other side of the world. Before the dawn the papers are carried forth. They hasten on glimmering trains out through the dark. Soon the newsboys shrill in the streets—China and the Philippines and Australia, and East and West they cry—the voices of the nations of the earth, and in my soul I worship the body of the man. Have I not seen two trains full of the will of the body of the man meet at full speed in the darkness of the night? I have watched them on the trembling ground—the flash of light, the crash of power, ninety miles an hour twenty inches apart, … thundering aisles of souls … on into blackness, and in my soul I worship the body of the man.

And when I go forth at night, feel the earth walking silently across heaven beneath my feet, I know that the heart-beat and the will of the man is in it—in all of it. With thousands of trains under it, over it, around it, he thrills it through with his will. I no longer look, since I have known this, upon the sun alone, nor upon the countenance of the hills, nor feel the earth around me growing softly or resting in the light, lifting itself to live. All that is, all that reaches out around me, is the body of the man. One must look up to stars and beyond horizons to look in his face. Who is there, I have said, that shall trace upon the earth the footsteps of this body, all wireless telegraph and steel, or know the sound of its going? Now, when I see it, it is a terrible body, trembling the earth. Like a low thunder it reaches around the crust of it, grasping it. And now it is a gentle body (oh, Signor Marconi!), swift as thought up over the hill of the sea, soft and stately as the walking of the clouds in the upper air.

Is there any one to-day so small as to know where he is? I am always coming suddenly upon my body, crying out with joy like a child in the dark, "And I am here, too!"

Has the twentieth century, I have wondered, a man in it who shall feel Himself?

And so it has come to pass, this vision I have seen with my own eyes—Man, my Brother, with his mean, absurd little unfinished body, going triumphant up and down the earth making limbs of Time and Space. Who is there who has not seen it, if only through the peephole of a dream—the whole earth lying still and strange in the hollow of his hand, the sea waiting upon him? Thousands of times I have seen it, the whole earth with a look, wrapped white and still in its ball of mist, the glint of the Atlantic on it, and in the blue place the vision of the ships.

Between the seas and skies

The Shuttle flies

Seven sunsets long, tropic-deep,

Thousand-sailed,

Half in waking, half in sleep.

Glistening calms and shouting gales

Water-gold and green,

And many a heavenly-minded blue

It thrusts and shudders through,

Past my starlight,

Past the glow of suns I know,

Weaving fates,

Loves and hates

In the Sea—

The stately Shuttle

To and fro,

Mast by mast,

Through the farthest bounds of moons and noons.

Flights of Days and Nights

Flies fast.

It may be true, as the poets are telling us, that this fashion the modern man has, of reaching out with steel and vapor and smoke, and holding a star silently in his hand, has no poetry in it, and that machinery is not a fit subject for poets. Perhaps. I am merely judging for myself. I have seen the few poets of this modern world crowded into their corner of it (in Westminster Abbey), and I have seen also a great foundry chiming its epic up to the night, freeing the bodies and the souls of men around the world, beating out the floors of cities, making the limbs of the great ships silently striding the sea, and rolling out the roads of continents.

If this is not poetry, it is because it is too great a vision. And yet there are times I am inclined to think when it brushes against us—against all of us. We feel Something there. More than once I have almost touched the edge of it. Then I have looked to see the man wondering at it. But he puts up his hands to his eyes, or he is merely hammering on something. Then I wish that some one would be born for him, and write a book for him, a book that should come upon the man and fold him in like a cloud, breathe into him where his wonder is. He ought to have a book that shall be to him like a whole Age—

the one he lives in, coming to him and leaning over him, whispering to him, "Rise, my Son and live. Dost thou not behold thy hands and thy feet?"

The trains like spirits flock to him.

There are days when I can read a time-table. When I put it back in my pocket it sings.

In the time-table I carry in my pocket I unfold the earth.

I have come to despise poets and dreams. Truths have made dreams pale and small. What is wanted now is some man who is literal enough to tell the truth.

II

THE IDEA OF SIZE

Sometimes I have a haunting feeling that the other readers of Mount Tom (besides me) may not be so tremendously interested after all in machinery and interpretations of machinery. Perhaps they are merely being polite about the subject while up here with me on the mountain, not wanting to interrupt exactly and not talking back. It is really no place for talking back, perhaps they think, on a mountain. But the trouble is, I get more interested than other people before I know it. Then suddenly it occurs to me to wonder if they are listening particularly and are not looking off at the scenery and the river and the hills and the meadow while I wander on about railroad trains and symbolism and the Mount Tom Pulp Mill and socialism and electricity and Schopenhauer and the other things, tracking out relations. It gets worse than other people's genealogies.

But all I ask is, that when they come, as they are coming now, just over the page to some more of these machine ideas, or interpretations as one might call them, or impressions, or orgies with engines, they will not drop the matter altogether. They may not feel as I do. It would be a great disappointment to all of us, perhaps, if I could be agreed with by everybody; but boring people is a serious matter—boring them all the time, I mean. It's no more than fair, of course, that the subscribers to a magazine should run some of the risk—as well as the editor—but I do like to think that in these next few pages there are—spots, and that people will keep hopeful.

Some people are very fond of looking up at the sky, taking it for a regular exercise, and thinking how small they are. It relieves them. I do not wish to deny that there is a certain luxury in it. But I must say that for all practical purposes of a mind—of having a mind—I would be willing to throw over whole hours and days of feeling very small, any time, for a single minute of feeling big. The details are more interesting. Feeling small, at best, is a kind of glittering generality.

I do not think I am altogether unaware how I look from a star—at least I have spent days and nights practising with a star, looking down from it on the thing I have agreed for the time being (whatever it is) to call myself, and I have discovered that the real luxury for me does not consist in feeling very small or even in feeling very large. The luxury for me is in having a regular reliable feeling, every day of my life, that I have been made on purpose— and very conveniently made, to be infinitely small or infinitely large as I like. I arrange it any time. I find myself saying one minute, "Are not the whole human race my house-servants? Is not London my valet—always at my door to do my bidding? Clouds do my errands for me. It takes a world to make room for my body. My soul is furnished with other worlds I cannot see."

The next minute I find myself saying nothing. The whole star I am on is a bit of pale yellow down floating softly through space. What I really seem to enjoy is a kind of insured feeling. Whether I am small or large all space cannot help waiting upon me—now that I have taken iron and vapor and light and made hands for my hands, millions of them, and reached out with them. A little one shall become a thousand. I have abolished all size—even my own size does not exist. If all the work that is being done by the hands of my hands had literally to be done by men, there would not be standing room for them on the globe—comfortable standing room. But even though, as it happens, much of the globe is not very good to stand on, and vast tracts of it, every year, are going to waste, it matters nothing to us. Every thing we touch is near or far, or large or small, as we like. As long as a young woman can sit down by a loom which is as good as six hundred more just like her, and all in a few square feet—as long as we can do up the whole of one of Napoleon's armies in a ball of dynamite, or stable twelve thousand horses in the boiler of an ocean steamer, it does not make very much difference what kind of a planet we are on, or how large or small it is. If suddenly it sometimes seems as if it were all used up and things look cramped again (which they do once in so often) we have but to think of something, invent something, and let it out a little. We move over into a new world in a minute. Columbus was mere bagatelle. We get continents every few days. Thousands of men are thinking of them—adding them on. Mere size is getting to be old-fashioned—as a way of arranging things. It has never been a very big earth— at best—the way God made it first. He made a single spider that could weave a rope out of her own body around it. It can be ticked all through, and all around, with the thoughts of a man. The universe has been put into a little telescope and the oceans into a little compass. Alice in Wonderland's romantic and clever way with a pill is become the barest matter of fact. Looking at the world a single moment with a soul instead of a theodolite, no one who has ever been on it—before—would know it. It's as if the world were a little wizened balloon that had been given us once and had been used so for thousands of years, and we had just lately discovered how to blow it.

III

THE IDEA OF LIBERTY

Some one told me one morning not so very long ago that the sun was getting a mile smaller across every ten years. It gave me a shut-in and helpless feeling. I found myself several times during that day looking at it anxiously. I almost held my hands up to it to warm them. I knew in a vague fashion that it would last long enough for me. And a mile in ten years was not much. It did not take much figuring to see that I had not the slightest reason to be anxious. But my feelings were hurt. I felt as if something had hit the universe. I could not get myself—and I have not been able to get myself since—to look at it impersonally. I suppose every man lives in some theory of the universe, unconsciously, every day, as much as he lives in the sunlight. And he does not want it disturbed. I have always felt safe before. And, what was a necessary part of safety with me, I have felt that history was safe—that there was going to be enough of it.

I have been in the world a good pleasant while on the whole, tried it and got used to it—used to the weather on it and used to having my friends hate me and my enemies turn on me and love me, and the other uncertainties; but all the time, when I looked up at the sun and saw it, or thought of it down under the world, I counted on it. I discovered that my soul had been using it daily as a kind of fulcrum for all things. I helped God lift with it. It was obvious that it was going to be harder for both of us—a mere matter of time. I could not get myself used to the thought. Every fresh look I took at the sun peeling off mile after mile up there, as fast as I lived, flustered me—made my sky less useful to me, less convenient to rest in. I found myself trying slowly to see how this universe would look—what it would be like, if I were the last man on it. Somebody would have to be. It would be necessary to justify things for him. He would probably be too tired and cold to do it. So I tried.

I had a good deal the same experience with Mount Pelée last summer. I resented being cooped up helplessly, on a planet that leaked.

The fact that it leaked several thousand miles away, and had made a comparatively safe hole for it, out in the middle of the sea, only afforded momentary relief. The hurt I felt was deeper than that. It could not be remedied by a mere applying long distances to it. It was underneath down in my soul. Time and Space could not get at it. The feeling that I had been trapped in a planet somehow, and that I could not get off possibly, the feeling that I had been deliberately taken body and soul, without my knowing it and without my ever having been asked, and set down on a cooled-off cinder to live, whether I wanted to or not—the sudden new appalling sense I had, that the ground underneath my feet was not really good and solid, that I was living every day of my life just over a roar of great fire, that I was being asked (and everybody else) to make history and build stone houses, and found institutions and things on the bare outside—the destroyed and ruined part of a ball that had been tossed out in space to burn itself up—the sense, on top of all this, that this dried crust I live on, or bit of caked ashes, was liable to break through suddenly at any time and pour down the center of the earth on one's head, did not add to the dignity, it seemed to me, or the self-respect of human life. "You might as well front the facts, my dear youth, look Mount Pelée in the face," I tried to say coldly and calmly to myself. "Here you are, set down helplessly among stars, on a great round blue and green something all fire and wind inside. And it is all liable—this superficial crust or geological ice you are on—perfectly liable, at any time or any place after this, to let through suddenly and dump all the nations and all ancient and modern history, and you and Your Book, into this awful ceaseless abyss—of boiled mountains and stewed up continents that is seething beneath your feet."

It is hard enough, it seems to me, to be an optimist on the edge of this earth as it is, to keep on believing in people and things on it, without having to believe besides that the earth is a huge round swindle just of itself, going round and round through all heaven, with all of us on it, laughing at us.

I felt chilled through for a long time after Mount Pelée broke out. I went wistfully about sitting in sunny and windless places trying to get warmed all summer. And it was not all in my soul. It was not all subjective. I noticed that the thermometer was caught the same way. It was a plain case enough—it seemed to me—the heater I lived on had let through, spilled out and wasted a lot of its fire, and the ground simply could not get warmed up after it. I sat in the sun and pictured the earth freezing itself up slowly and deliberately, on the outside. I had it all arranged in my mind. The end of the world was not coming as the ancients saw it, by a kind of overflow of fire, but by the fires going out. A mile off the sun every ten years (this for the loss of outside heat) and volcanoes and things (for the inside heat), and gradually between being frozen under us, and frozen over us, both, both sides at once, the human race would face the situation. We would have to learn to live together. Any one could see that. The human race was going to be one long row, sometime—great nations of us and little ones all at last huddled up along the equator to keep warm. Just outside of this a little way, it would be perfectly empty star, all in a swirl of snowdrifts.

I do not claim that it was very scientific to feel in this way, but I have always had, ever since I can remember, a moderate or decent human interest in the universe as a universe, and I had always felt as if the earth had made, for all practical purposes, a sort of contract with the human race, and when it acted like this—cooled itself off all of a sudden, in the middle of a hot summer, and all to show off a comparatively unknown and unimportant mountain hid on an island far out at sea—I could not conceal from myself (in my present and usual capacity as a kind of agent or sponsor for humanity) that there was something distinctly jarring about it and disrespectful. I felt as if we had been trifled with. It was not a feeling I had very long—this injured feeling toward the universe in behalf of the man in it, but I could not help it at first. There grew an anger within me and then out of the anger a great delight. It seemed to me I saw my soul standing afar off down there, on its cold and emptied-looking earth.

Then slowly I saw it was the same soul I had always had. I was standing as I had always stood on an earth before, be it a bare or flowering one. I saw myself standing before all that was. Then I defied the heaven over my head and the ground under my feet not to keep me strong and glad before God. I saw that it mattered not to me, of an earth, how bare it was, or could be, or could be made to be; if the soul of a man could be kept burning on it, victory and gladness would be alive upon it. I fell to thinking of the man. I took an inventory down in my being of all that the man was, of the might of the spirit that was in him. Would it be anything new to the man to be maltreated, a little, neglected—almost outwitted by a universe? Had he not already, thousands of times in the history of this planet, flung his spirit upon the cold, and upon empty space—and made homes out of it? He had snuggled in icebergs. He had entered the place of the mighty heat and made the coolness of shadow out of it.

It was nothing new. The planet had always been a little queer. It was when it commenced. The only difference would seem to be that, instead of having the earth at first the way it is going to be by and by apparently—an earth with a little rim of humanity around it, great nations toeing the equator to live—everything was turned around. All the young nations might have been seen any day crowded around the ends or tips of the earth to keep from falling into the fire that was still at work on the middle of it, finishing it off and getting it ready to have things happen on it. Boys might have been seen almost any afternoon, in those early days, going out to the north pole and playing duck on the rock to keep from being too warm.

It is a mere matter of opinion or of taste—the way a planet acts at any given time. Now it is one way and now another, and we do as we like.

I do not pretend to say in so many words if the sun grew feeble, just what the man would do, down in his snowdrifts. But I know he would make some kind of summer out of them. One cannot help feeling that if the sun went out, it would be because he wanted it to—had arranged something, if nothing but a good bit of philosophy. It is not likely that the man has defied the heavens and the earth all these centuries for nothing. The things they have done against him have been the making of him. When he found this same sun we are talking about, in the earliest days of all, was a sun that kept running away from him and left him in a great darkness half of every day he lived, he knew what to do. Every time that Heaven has done anything to him, he has had his answer ready. The man who finds himself on a planet that is only lighted part of the time, is merely reminded that he must think of something. He digs light out of the ground and glows up the world with her own sap. When he finds himself living on an earth that can only be said to be properly heated a small fraction of the year, he makes the earth itself to burn itself and keep him warm. Things like this are small to us. We put coal through a desire and take the breath out of its dark body, and put it in pipes, and cook our food with poisons. We take water and burn it into air and we telegraph boilers, and flash mills around the earth on poles. We move vast machines with a little throb, like light. We put a street on a wire. Great crowds in the great cities—whole blocks of them—are handed along day and night like dots and dashes in telegrams. A man cannot be stopped by a breath. We save a man up in his own whisper hundreds of years when he is dead. A human voice that reaches only a few yards makes thousands of miles of copper talk. Then we make the thousand miles talk without the copper wire. We stand on the shore and beat the air with a thought thousands of miles away—make it whisper for us to ships. One need not fear for a man like this—a man who has made all the earth a deed, an action of his own soul, who has thrown his soul at last upon the waste of heaven and made words out of it. One cannot but believe that a man like this is a free man. Let what will happen to the sun that warms him or the star that seems just now his foothold in space. All shall be as his soul says when his soul determines what it shall say. Fire and wind and cold—when his soul speaks—and Invisibility itself and Nothing are his servants.

The vision of a little helpless human race huddled in the tropics saying its last prayers, holding up its face to a far-off neglected-looking universe, warming its hands at the stars—the vision of all the great peoples of the earth squeezed up into Esquimaux, in furs up to their eyes, stamping their feet on the equator to keep warm, is merely the sort of vision that one set of scientists gloats on giving us. One needs but to look for what the other set is saying. It has not time to be saying much, but what it practically says is: "Let the sun wizen up if it wants to. There will be something. Somebody will think of something. Possibly we are outgrowing suns. At all events to a real man any little accident or bruise to the planet he's on is a mere suggestion of how strong he is. Some new beautiful impossibility—if the truth were known—is just what we are looking for."

A human race which makes its car wheels and napkins out of paper, its street pavements out of glass, its railway ties out of old shoes, which draws food out of air, which winds up operas on spools, which has its way with oceans, and plays chess with the empty ether that is over the sea—which makes clouds speak with tongues, which lights railway trains with pin-wheels and which makes its cars go by stopping them, and heats its furnaces with smoke—it would be very strange if a race like this could not find some way at least of managing its own planet, and (heaped with snowdrifts though it be) some way of warming it, or of melting off a place to live on. A corporation was formed down in New Jersey the other day to light a city by the tossing of the waves. We are always getting some new grasp—giving some new sudden almost humorous stretch to matter. We keep nature fairly smiling at herself. One can hardly tell, when one hears of half the new things nowadays—actual facts—whether to laugh or cry, or form a stock company or break out into singing. No one would dare to say that a thousand years from now we will not have found some other use for moonlight than for love affairs and to haul tides with. We will be manufacturing noon yet, out of compressed starlight, and heating houses with it. It will be peddled about the streets like milk, from door to door in cases and bottles.

First and last, whatever else may be said of us, we do as we like with a planet. Nothing it can do to us, nothing that can happen to it, outwits us—at least more than a few hundred years at a time. The idea that we cannot even keep warm on it is preposterous. Nothing would be more likely—almost any time now—than for some one to decide that we ought to have our continents warmed more, winters. It would not be much, as things are going, to remodel the floors of a few of our continents—put in registers and things, have the heat piped up from the center of the earth. The best way to get a faint idea of what science is going to be like the next few thousand years, is to pick out something that could not possibly be so and believe it. We manufacture ice in July by boiling it, and if we cannot warm a planet as we want to—at least a few furnished continents—with hot things, we will do it with cold ones, or by rubbing icebergs together. If one wants a good simple working outfit for a prophet in science and mechanics, all one has to do is to think of things that are unexpected enough, and they will come to pass. A scientist out in the Northwest has just finished his plans for getting hold of the other end of the force of gravity. The general idea is to build a sort of tower or flag-pole on the planet—something that reaches far enough out over the edge to get an underhold as it were—grip hold of the force of gravity where it works backwards. Of course, as anyone can see at a glance, when it is once built out with steel, the first forty miles or so (workmen using compressed air and tubular trolleys, etc.), everything on the tower would pull the other way and the pressure would gradually be relieved until the thing balanced itself. When completed it could be used to draw down electricity from waste space (which has as much as everybody on this planet could ever want, and more). What a little earth like ours would develop into, with a connection like this—a sort of umbilical cord to the infinite—no one would care to try to say. It would at least be a kind of planet that would always be sure of anything it wanted. When we had used up all the raw material or live force in our own world we could draw on the others. At the very least we would have a sort of signal station to the planets in general that would be useful. They would know what we want, and if we could not get it from them they would tell us where we could.

All this may be a little mixing perhaps. It is always difficult to tell the difference between the sublime and the ridiculous in talking of a being like man. It is what makes him sublime—that there is no telling about him—that he is a great, lusty, rollicking, easy-going son of God and throws off a world every now and then, or puts one on, with quips and jests. When the laugh dies away his jokes are prophecies. It behooves us therefore to walk softly, you and I, Gentle Reader, while we are here with him—while this dear gentle ground is still beneath our feet. There is no telling his reach. Let us notice stars more.

In the meantime it does seem to me that a comparatively simple affair like this one single planet, need not worry us much.

I still keep seeing it—I cannot help it—I always keep seeing it—eternities at a time, warm, convenient, and comfortable, the same old green and white, with all its improvements on it, whatever the sun does. And above all I keep seeing the Man on it, full of defiance and of love and worship, being born and buried—the little-great man, running about and strutting, flying through space on it, all his interests and his loves wound about it like clouds, but beckoning to worlds as he flies. And whatever the Man does with the other worlds or with this one, I always keep seeing this one, the same old stand or deck in eternity, for praying and singing and living, it always was. Long after I am dead, oh, dear little planet, least and furthest breath that is blown on thy face, my soul flocks to you, rises around you, and looks back upon you and watches you down there in your round white cloud, rowing faithfully through space!

IV

THE IDEA OF IMMORTALITY

If I had never thought of it before, and some one were to come around to my study tomorrow morning and tell me that I was immortal, I am not at all sure that I would be attracted by it. The first thing that I should do, probably, would be to argue a little—ask him what it was for. I might take some pains not to commit myself (one does not want to settle a million years in a few minutes), but I cannot help being conscious, on the inside of my own mind, at least, that the first thought on immortality that would come to me, would be that perhaps it might be overdoing things a little.

I can speak only for myself. I am not unaware that a great many men and women are talking to-day about immortality and writing about it. I know many people too, who, in a faithful, worried way seem to be lugging about with them, while they live, what they call a faith in immortality. I would not mean to say a word against immortality, if I were asked suddenly and had never thought of it before. If by putting out my hand I could get some of it, for other people,—people that wanted it or thought they did—I would probably. They would be happier and easier to live with. I could watch them enjoying the idea of how long they were going to last. There would be a certain social pleasure in it. But, speaking strictly for myself, if I were asked suddenly and had never heard of it before, I would not have the slightest preference on the subject. It may be true, as some say, that a man is only half alive if he does not long to live forever, but while I have the best wishes and intentions with regard to my hope for immortality I cannot get interested. I feel as if I were living forever now, this very moment, right here on the premises—Universe, Earth, United States of America, Hampshire County, Northampton, Massachusetts. I feel infinitely related every day and hour and minute of my life, to an infinite number of things. As for joggling God's elbow or praying to Him or any such thing as that, under the circumstances, and begging Him to let me live forever, it always seems to me (I have done it sometimes when I was very tired) as if it were a way of denying Him to His face. How a man who is literally standing up to his soul's eyes, and to the tops of the stars in the infinite, who can feel the eternal throbbing through the very pores of his body, can so far lose his sense of humor in a prayer, or his reverence in it, as to put up a petition to God to live forever, I entirely fail to see. I always feel as if I had stopped living forever—to ask Him.

I have traveled in the blaze of a trolley car when all the world was asleep, and have been shot through still country fields in the great blackness. All things that were—it seemed to my soul, were snuffed out. It was as if all the earth had become a whir and a bit of light—had dwindled away to a long plunge, or roll and roar through Nothing. Slowly as I came to myself I said, "Now I will try to realize Motion. I will see if I can know. I spread my soul about me…." Ties flying under my feet, black poles picked out with lights, flapping ghostlike past the windows…. Voices of wheels over and under…. The long, dreary waver of the something that sounds when the car stops (and which feels like taking gas) … the semi-confidential, semi-public talk of the passengers, the sudden collision with silence, they come to, when the car halts—all these. Finally when I look up every one has slipped away. Then I find my soul spreading further and further. The great night, silent and splendid, builds itself over me. The night is the crowded time to travel—car almost to one's self, nothing but a few whirls of light and a conductor for company—the long monotone of miles—miles—flying beside me and above and around and beneath—all this shadowed world to belong to, to dwell in, to pick out with one's soul from Darkness. "Here am I," I said as the roar tightened once more, and gripped on its awful wire and glowed through the blackness. "Here I am in infinite space, I and my bit of glimmer…. Worlds fall about me. The very one I am on, and stamp my feet on to know it is there, falls and plunges with me out through deserts of space, and stars I cannot see have their hand upon me and hold me."

No one would deny that the idea of immortality is a well-meaning idea and pleasantly inclined and intended to be appreciative of a God, but it does seem to me that it is one of the most absent-minded ways of appreciating Him that could be conceived. I am infinite at 88 High Street. I have all the immortality I can use, without going through my own front gate. I have but to look out of a window. There is no denying that Mount Tom is convenient, and as a kind of soul-stepping-stone, or horse-block to the infinite, the immeasurable and immortal, a mountain may be an advantage, perhaps, and make some difference; but I must confess that it seems to me that in all times and in all places a man's immortality is absolutely in his own hands. His immortality consists in his being in an immortally related state of mind. His immortality is his sense of having infinite relations with all the time there is, and his infinity consists in his having infinite relations with all the space there is. Wherever, as a matter of form, a man may say he is living or staying, the universe is his real address.

I have been at sea—lain with a board over me out in the wide night and looked at the infinite through a port-hole. Over the edge of the swash of a wave I have gathered in oceans and possessed them. Under my board in the night I have lain still with the whole earth and mastered it in my heart, shared it until I could not sleep with the joy of it—the great ship with all its souls throbbing a planet through me and chanting it to me. I thought to my soul, "Where art thou?" I looked down upon myself as if I were a God looking down on myself and upon the others, and upon the ship and upon the waters.

A thousand breaths we lie

Shrouded limbs and faces

Horizontal

Packed in cases

In our named and numbered places,

Catalogued for sleep,

Trembling through the Godlight

Below, above,

Deep to Deep.

How a church-going man in a world like this can possibly contrive to have time to cry out or worry on it, or to be troubled about another—how he can demand another, the way he does sometimes, as if it were the only thing left a God could do to straighten matters out for having put him on this one, and how he can call this religion—is a problem that leaves my mind like an exhausted receiver. It is a grave question whether any immortality they are likely to get in another world would ever really pay some people for the time they have wasted in this one, worrying about it.

Does any science in the world suppose or dare to suppose that I am as unimportant in it as I look—or that I could be if I tried? that I am a parasite rolled up in a drop of dew, down under a shimmering mist of worlds that do not serve me nor care for me? I swear daily that I am not living and that I will not and cannot live underneath a universe … with a little horizon or teacup of space set down over me. The whole sky is the tool of my daily life. It belongs to me and I to it. I have said to the heavens that they shall hourly minister to me—to the uses of my spirit and the needs of my body. When I, or my spirit, would move a little I swing out on stars. In the watches of the night they reach under my eyelids and serve my sleep and wait on me with dreams, I know I am immortal because I know I am infinite. A man is at least as long as he is wide. There is no need to quibble with words. I care little enough whether I am supposed to say it is forever across my soul or everywhere across it. Whichever it is, I make it the other when I am ready. If a man is infinite and lives an infinitely related life, why should it matter whether he is eternal as he calls it or not,—takes his immortality sideways here, now, and in the terms of space or later with some kind of time-arrangement stretched out and petering along over a long, narrow row of years?

Thousands of things are happening that are mine—out, around, and through the great darkness—being born and killed and ticked and printed while I sleep. When I have stilled myself with sleep, do I not know that the lightning is waiting on me? When I see a cloud of steam I say, "There is my omnipresence." My being is busy out in the universe having its way somewhere. The days on the other side of the world are my days. I get what I want out of them without having to keep awake for them. In the middle of the night and without trying I lay my hand on the moon. It is my moon, wherever it may be, or whether I so much as look upon it, and when I do look upon it it is no roof for me, and the stars behind it flow in my veins.

II

I have been reading lately a book on Immortality, the leading idea of which seems to be a sort of astral body for people—people who are worthy of it. The author does not believe after the old-fashioned method that we are going to the stars. He intimates (for all practical purposes) that we do not need to. The stars are coming to us,—are already being woven in us. The author does not say it in so many words, but the general idea seems to be that the more spiritual or subtle body we are going to have, is already started in us—if we live as we should—growing like a kind of lining for this one.

I can only speak for one, but I find that when I am willing to take the time from reading books on immortality to enjoy a few infinite experiences, I am not apt to be troubled very much about another world.

It is daily obvious to me that I belong and that I am living in an infinite and eternal world, inconceivably better planned and managed than one of mine would be, and the only logical thing that I can do, is to take it for granted that the next one is even better than this. If the main feature of the next world consists in there not being one, then so much the better. I would not have thought so. It seems a little abrupt at this moment, perhaps, but it is a mere detail and why not leave it to God to work it out? He doesn't have to neglect anything to do it—which is what we do—and He is going to do it anyway.

I have refused to take time from my infinity now for a theory of a theory about some new kind by and by. I have but to stand perfectly still. There is an infinite opening and shutting of doors for me, through all the heavens and the earth. I lie with my head in the deep grass. A square yard is forever across. I listen to a great city in the grass—millions of insects. Microscopes have threaded it for me. I know their city—all its mighty little highways. I possess it. And when I walk away I rebuild their city softly in my heart. Winds, tides, and vapors are for me everywhere, that my soul may possess them. I reach down to the silent metals under my feet that millions of ages have worked on, and fire and wonder and darkness. I feel the sun and the lives of nations flowing around to me, from under the sea. Who can shut me out from anybody's sunrise?

"Oh, tenderly the haughty day

Fills his blue urn with fire;

One morn is in the mighty heaven

And one in my desire."

I play with the Seasons, with all the weathers on earth. I can telegraph for them. I go to the weather I want. The sky—to me—is no longer a great, serious, foreign-looking shore, conducting a big foolish cloud-business, sending down decrees of weather on helpless cities. With a whistle and a roar I defy it—move any strip of it out from over me—for any other strip. I order the time of year. It is my sky. I bend it a little—just a little. The sky no longer has a monopoly of wonder. With the hands of my hands, my brother and I have made an earth that can answer a sky back, that can commune with a sky. The soul at last guesses at its real self. It reaches out and dares. Men go about singing with telescopes. I do not always need to lift my hands to a sky and pray to it now. I am related to it. With the hands of my hands I work with it. I say "I and the sky." I say "I and the Earth." We are immortal because we are infinite. We have reached over with the hands of our hands. They are praying a stupendous prayer—a kind of god's prayer. God's hand has been grasped—vaguely—wonderfully out in the Dark. No longer is the joy of the universe to a man, one of his great, solemn, solitary joys. The sublime itself is a neighborly thought. God's machine—up—There—and the machines of the man have signaled each other.

V

THE IDEA OF GOD

My study (not the place where I get my knowledge but the place where I put it together) is a great meadow—ten square splendid level miles of it—as fenceless and as open as a sky—merely two mountains to stand guard. If H—— the scientist who lives nearest to me (that is; nearest to my mind,) were to come down to me to-morrow morning, down in my meadow, with its huge triangle of trolleys and railways humming gently around the edges and tell me that he had found a God, I would not believe it. "Where?" I would say, "in which Bottle?" I have groped for one all these years. Ever since I was a child I have been groping for a God. I thought one had to. I have turned over the pages of ancient books and hunted in morning papers and rummaged in the events of the great world and looked on the under sides of leaves and guessed on the other sides of the stars and all in vain. I never could make out to find a God in that way. I wonder if anyone can.

I know it is not the right spirit to have, but I must confess that when the scientist (the smaller sort of scientist around the corner in my mind and everybody's mind) with all his retorts and things, pottering with his argument of design, comes down to me in my meadow and reminds me that he has been looking for a God and tells me cautiously and with all his kind, conscientious hems and haws that he has found Him, I wonder if he has.

The very necessity a man is under of seeking a God at all, in a world alive all over like this, of feeling obliged to go on a long journey to search one out makes one doubt if the kind of God he would find would be worth while. I have never caught a man yet who has found his God in this way, enjoying Him or getting anyone else to.

It does seem to me that the idea of a God is an absolutely plain, rudimentary, fundamental, universal human instinct, that the very essence of finding a God consists in His not having to be looked for, in giving one's self up to one's plain every-day infinite experiences. I suppose if it could be analyzed, the poet's real quarrel with the scientist is not that he is material, but that he is not material enough,—he does not conceive matter enough to find a God. I cannot believe for instance that any man on earth to whom the great spectacle of matter going on every day before his eyes is a scarcely noticed thing—any man who is willing to turn aside from this spectacle—this spectacle as a whole—and who looks for a God like a chemist in a bottle for instance—a bottle which he places absolutely by itself, would be able to find one if he tried. It seems to me that it is by letting one's self have one's infinite—one's infinitely related experiences, and not by cutting them off that one comes to know a God. To find a God who is everywhere one must at least spend a part of one's time in being everywhere one's self—in relating one's knowledge to all knowledge.

There are various undergirding arguments and reasons, but the only way that I really know there is an infinite God is because I am infinite—in a small way—myself. Even the matter that has come into the world connected with me, and that belongs to me, is infinite. If my soul, like some dim pale light left burning within me, were merely to creep to the boundaries of its own body, it would know there was a God. The very flesh I live with every day is infinite flesh. From the furthest rumors of men and women, the furthest edge of time and space my soul has gathered dust to itself. I carry a temple about with me. If I could do no better, and if there were need, I am my own cathedral. I worship when I breathe. I bow down before the tick of my pulse. I chant to the palm of my hand. The lines in the tips of my fingers could not be duplicated in a million years. Shall any man ask me to prove there are miracles or to put my finger on God? or to go out into some great breath of emptiness or argument to be sure there is a God? I am infinite. Therefore there is a God. I feel daily the God within me. Has He not kindled the fire in my bones and out of the burning dust warmed me before the stars—made a hearth for my soul before them? I am at home with them. I sit daily before worlds as at my own fireside.

I suppose there is something intolerant and impatient and a little heartless about an optimist—especially the kind of optimism that is based upon a simple everyday rudimentary joy in the structure of the world. There is such a thing, I suppose, with some of us, as having a kind of devilish pride in faith, as one would say to ordinary mortals and creepers and considerers and arguers "Oh now just see me believe!" We are like boys taking turns jumping in the Great Vacant Lot, seeing which can believe the furthest. We need to be reminded that a man cannot simply bring a little brag to God, about His world, and make a religion out of it. I do not doubt in the least, as a matter of theory, that I have the wrong spirit—sometimes—toward the scientific man who lives around the corner of my mind. It seems to me he is always suggesting important-looking unimportant things. I have days of sympathizing with him, of rolling his great useless heavy-empty pack up upon my shoulders and strapping it there. But before I know it I'm off. I throw it away or melt it down into a tablet or something—put it in my pocket. I walk jauntily before God.

And the worst of it is, I think He intended me to. I think He intended me to know and to keep knowing daily what He has done for me and is doing now, out in the universe, and what He has made me to do. I also am a God. From the first time I saw the sun I have been one daily. I have performed daily all the homelier miracles and all the common functions of a God. I have breathed the Invisible into my being. Out of the air of heaven I have made flesh. I have taken earth from the earth and burned it within me and made it into prayers and into songs. I have said to my soul "To eat is to sing." I worship all over. I am my own sacrament. I lay before God nights of sleep, and the delight and wonder of the flesh I render back to Him again, daily, as an offering in His sight.

And what is true of my literal body—of the joy of my hands and my feet, is still more true of the hands of my hands.

When I wake in the night and send forth my thought upon the darkness, track out my own infinity in it, feel my vast body of earth and sky reaching around me, all telegraphed through with thought, and floored with steel, I may have to grope for a God a little (I do sometimes), but I do it with loud cheers. I sing before the door of heaven if there is a heaven or needs to be a heaven. When I look upon the glory of the other worlds, has not science itself told me that they are a part of me and I a part of them? Nothing is that would not be different without something else. My thoughts are ticking through the clouds, and the great sun itself is creeping through me daily down in my bones. The steam cloud hurries for me on a hundred seas. I turn over in my sleep at midnight and lay my hand on the noon. And when I have slept and walk forth in the morning, the stars flow in my veins. Why should a man dare to whine? "Whine not at me!" I have said to man my brother. If you cannot sing to me do not interrupt me.

Let him sing to me

Who sees the watching of the stars above the day,

Who hears the singing of the sunrise

On its way

Through all the night.

Who outfaces skies, outsings the storms,

Whose soul has roamed

Infinite-homed

Through tents of Space,

His hand in the dim Great Hand that forms

All wonder.

Let him sing to me

Who is The Sky Voice, The Thunder Lover

Who hears above the wind's fast-flying shrouds

The drifted darkness, the heavenly strife,

The singing on the sunny sides of all the clouds,

Of His Own Life.

VI

THE IDEA OF THE UNSEEN AND INTANGIBLE

AN ODE TO THE UNSEEN

Poets of flowers, singers of nooks in Space,

Petal-mongers, embroiderers of words

In the music-haunted houses of the birds,

Singers with the thrushes and pewees

In the glimmer-lighted roofs

Of the trees—

Unhand my soul!

Buds with singing in their hearts,

Birds with blooms upon their wings,

All the wandering whispers of delight,

The near familiar things;

Voice of pine trees, winds of daisies,

Sounds of going in the grain

Shall not bind me to thy singing

When the sky with God is ringing

For the Joy of the Rain.

Sea and star and hill and thunder,

Dawn and sunset, noon and night,

All the vast processional of the wonder

Where the worlds are,

Where my soul is,

Where the shining tracks are

For the spirit's flight—

Lift thine eyes to these

From the haunts of dewdrops,

Hollows of the flowers,

Caves of bees

That sing like thee,

Only in their bowers;

From the stately growing cities

Of the little blowing leaves,

To the infinite windless eaves

Of the stars;

From the dainty music of the ground,

The dim innumerable sound

Of the Mighty Sun

Creeping in the grass,

Softest stir of His feet

(Where they go

Far and slow

On their immemorial beat

Of buds and seeds

And all the gentle and holy needs

Of flowers),

To the old eternal round

Of the Going of His Might,

Above the confines of the dark,

Odors and winds and showers,

Day and night,

Above the dream of death and birth

Flickering East and West,

Boundaries of a Shadow of an Earth—

Where He wheels

And soars

And plays

In illimitable light,

Sends the singing stars upon their ways

And on each and every world

When The Little Shadow for its Little Sleep

Is furled—

Pours the Days.

•   •   •

The first time I gazed in the great town upon a solid mile of electric cars—
threaded with Nothing—mesmerism hauling a whole city home to supper, it
seemed to me as if the central power of all things, The Thing that floats and
breathes through the universe, must have been found by someone—
gathered up from between stars, and turned on—poured down gently on the
planet—falling on a thousand wheels, and run on the tops of cars—the secret
thrill that softly and out in the darkness and through all ages had done all
things. I felt as if I had seen the infinite in some near familiar, humdrum
place. I walked on in a dazed fashion. I do not suppose I could really have
been more surprised if I had met a star walking in the street.

In my deepest dream

I heard the Song

Running in my sleep

Through the lowest caves of Being

Down below

Where no sound is, sun is,

Hearing, seeing

That men know.

There was something about it, about that sense of the mile of cars moving,
that made it all seem very old.

An Ode to the Lightning.

Before the first new dust of dream God took

For making man and hope and love and graves

Had kindled to its fate. Before the floods

Had folded round the hills. Before the rainbow

Born of cloud had taught the sky its tints,

The Lightning Minstrel was. The cry of Vague

To Vague. The Chaos-voice that rolled and crept

From out the pale bewildered wonder-stuff

That wove the worlds,

Before the Hand had stirred that touched them,

While still, hinged on nothing,

Dim and shapeless Things

And clouds with groping sleep upon their wings

Floated and waited.

Before the winds had breathed the breath of life

Or blown from wastes of Space

To Earth's creating place,

The souls of seeds

And ghosts of old dead stars,

The Lightning Spirit willed

Their feet with wonder should be thrilled.

—Primal fire of all desire

That leaps from men to men,

Brother of Suns

And all the Glorious Ones

That circle skies,

He flashed to these

The night that brought the birth,

The vision of the place

And raised his awful face

To all their glittering crowds,

And cried from where It lay

—A tiny ball of fire and clay

In swaddling clothes of clouds,

"Behold the Earth!"

   •   •   •   •   •   •   •

   •   •   •   •   •   •   •

Oh heavenly feet of The Hot Cloud! Bringer

Of the garnered airs. Herald of the shining rains!

Looser of the locked and lusty winds from their misty caves.

Opener of the thousand thousand-gloried doors twixt heaven

And heaven and Heaven's heaven. Oh thou whose play

Men make to do their work (*Why do their work?*)

—And call from holidays of space, sojourns

Of suns and moons, and lock to earth

(*Why lock to earth?*)

That the Dead Face may flash across the seas

The cry of the new-born babe be heard around

A world. Ah me! and the click of lust

And the madness and the gladness and the ache

Of Dust, Dust!

AN ODE TO THE TELEGRAPH WIRES.

THE SONG THE WORLD SANG LAYING THE ATLANTIC CABLE

The mortal wires of the heart of the earth

I sing, melted and fused by men,

That the immortal fires of their souls should fling

To eaves of heaven and caves of sea,

And God Himself, and farthest hills and dimmest bounds of sense

The flame of the Creature's ken,

The flame of the glow of the face of God

Upon the face of men.

Wind-singing wires
Along their thousand airy aisles,
Feet of birds and songs of leaves,
Glimmer of stars and dewy eves.
Sea-singing wires
Along their thousand slimy miles,
Shadowy deeps,
Unsunned steeps,
Beating in their awful caves
To mouthing fish and bones
And weeds unfurled
Deserts of waves
The heart-beat of this upper world.
Infinite blue, infinite green,
Infinite glory of the ear
Ticking its passions through
Infinite fear,
Ooze of storm, sodden and slanting wrecks
The forever untrodden decks
Of Death,
Ever the seething wires
On the floors
Of the world,
Below the last
Locked fast
Water-darkened doors
Of the sun,
Lighting the awful signal fires

Of our speechless vast desires

On the mountains and the hills

Of the sea

Till the sandy-buried heights

And the sullen sunken vales

And fire-defying barrens of the deep

The hearth of souls shall be

Beacons of Thought,

And from the lurk of the shark

To the sunrise-lighted eerie of the lark

And where the farthest cloud-sail fills

Shall be felt the throbbing and the sobbing and the hoping

The might and mad delight,

The hell-and-heaven groping

Of our little human wills.

AN ODE TO THE WIRELESS

THE PRAYER OF MAN THROUGH ALL THE YEARS IN WHICH THE SKY-TELEGRAPH WOULD NOT WORK

Roofed in with fears,

Beneath its little strip of sky

That is blown about

In and out

Across my wavering strip of years—

Who am I

Whose singing scarce doth reach

The cloud-climbed hills,

To take upon my lips the speech

Of those whose voices Heaven fills

With splendor?

And yet—

I cannot quite forget

That in the underdawn of dreams

I have felt the faint surmise

Shining through the starry deep of my sleep

That I with God went singing once

Up and down with suns and storms

Through the phantom-pillared forms

And stately-silent naves

And thunder-dreaming caves

Of Heaven.

Great Spirit—Thou who in my being's burning mesh

Hath wrought the shining of the mist through and through the flesh,

Who, through the double-wondered glory of the dust

Hast thrust

Habits of skies upon me, souls of days and nights,

Where are the deeds that needs must be,

The dreams, the high delights,

That I once more may hear my voice

From cloudy door to door rejoice—

May stretch the boundaries of love

Beyond the mumbling, mock horizons of my fears

To the faint-remembered glory of those years—

May lift my soul

And reach this Heaven of thine

With mine?

Where are the gleams?

Thou shalt tell me,

Shalt compel me.

The sometime glory shall return
I know.

The day shall be
When by wondering I shall learn
With vapor-fingers to discern
The music-hidden keys of skies—
Shall touch like thee
Until they answer me
The chords of the silent air
And strike the wild and slumber-music out
Dreaming there.
Above the hills of singing that I know
On the trackless, soundless path
That wonder hath
I shall go,
Beyond the street-cry of the poet,
The hurdy-gurdy singing
Of the throngs,
To the Throne of Silence,
Where the Doors
That guard the farthest faintest shores
Of Day
Swing their bars,
And shut the songs of heaven in
From all our dreaming-doing din,
Behind the stars.

There, at last,
The climbing and the singing passed,
And the cry,

My hushed and listening soul shall lie

At the feet of the place

Where the Singer sings

Who Hides His Face.

VII

THE IDEA OF GREAT MEN

"I had a vision under a green hedge

A hedge of hips and haws—Men yet shall hear

Archangels rolling over the high mountains

Old Satan's empty skull."

As it looks from MOUNT TOM, casting a general glance around, the Earth has about been put into shape, now, to do things.

The Earth has never been seen before looking so trim and convenient—so ready for action—as it is now. Steamships and looms and printing presses and railways have been supplied, wireless telegraph furnishings have lately been arranged throughout, and we have put in speaking tubes on nearly all the continents, and it looks—as seen from Mount Tom, at least, as if the planet were just being finished up, now, for a Great Author.

It is true that art and literature do not have, at first glance, a prosperous look in a machine age, but probably the real trouble the modern world is having with its authors is not because it is a world full of materialism and machinery, but because its authors are the wrong size.

The modern world as it booms along recognizes this, in its practical way, and instead of stopping to speak to its little authors, to its poets crying beside it, and stooping to them and encouraging them, it is quietly and sensibly (as it seems to some of us) going on with its machines and things making preparations for bigger ones.

I have thought the great authors in every age were made by the greatness of the listening to them. The greatest of all, I notice, have felt listened to by

God. Even the lesser ones (who have sometimes been called greatest) have felt listened to, most of them, one finds, by nothing less than nations. The man Jesus gathers kingdoms about Him in His talk, like an infant class. It was the way He felt. Almost any one who could have felt himself listened to in this daring way that Jesus did would have managed to say something. He could hardly have missed, one would think, letting fall one or two great ideas at least—ideas that nations would be born for.

It ought not to be altogether without meaning to a modern man that the great prophets and interpreters have talked as a rule to whole nations and that they have talked to them generally, too, for the glory of the whole earth. They could not get their souls geared smaller than a whole earth. Shakspeare feels the generations stretching away like galleries around him listening—when he makes love. It was no particular heroism or patience in the man Columbus that made him sail across an ocean and discover a continent. He had the girth of an earth in him and had to do something with it. He could not have helped it. He discovered America because he felt crowded.

One would think from the way some people have of talking or writing of immortality that it must be a kind of knack. As a matter of historic fact it has almost always been some mere great man's helplessness. When people have to be created and born on purpose, generation after generation of them, to listen to a man, two or three thousand years of them sometimes, on this planet, it is because the man himself when he spoke felt the need of them— and mentioned it. It is the man who is in the habit of addressing his remarks to a few continents and to several centuries who gets them.

I would not dare to say just how or when our next great author on this earth is going to happen to us, but I shall begin to listen hard and look expectant the first time I hear of a man who gets up on his feet somewhere in it and who speaks as if the whole earth were listening to him. If ever there was an earth that is getting ready to listen, and to listen all over, it is this one. And the first great man who speaks in it is going to speak as if he knew it. It is a world which has been allowed about a million years now, to get to the point where it could be said to begin to be conscious of being a world at all. And I cannot believe that a world which for the first time in its history has at last the conveniences for listening all over, if it wants to, is not going to produce at the same time a man who shall have something to say to it—a man that shall be worthy of the first single full audience, sunset to sunset, that has ever been thought of. It would seem as if, to say the least, such an audience as this, gathering half in light and half in darkness around a star, would celebrate by having a man to match. It would not be necessary for him to fall back, either, one would think, upon anything that has ever been said or thought of before. Already even in the sight and sounds of this present world has the verse of scripture about the next come true—"Eye hath not seen nor ear heard." It is not conceivable that there shall not be something said unspeakably and incredibly great to the first full house the planet has afforded.

I have gone to the place of books. I have seen before this all the peoples flocking past me under the earth with their little corner-saviors—each with his own little disc of worship all to himself on the planet—partitioned away from the rest for thousands of years. But now the whole face of the earth is changed. No longer can great men and great events be aimed at it and glanced off on it—into single nations. Great men, when they come now, can generally have a world at their feet. It is not possible that we shall not have them. The whole earth is the wager that we are going to have them. The bids are out—great statesmen, great actors, great financiers, great authors—even millionaires will gradually grow great. It cannot be helped. And it will be strange if someone cannot think of something to say, with the first full house this planet has afforded.

Even as it is now, let any man with a great girth of love in him but speak once—but speak one single round-the-world delight and nations sit at his feet. When Rudyard Kipling is dying with pneumonia seven seas listen to his breathing. The nations are in galleries on the stage of the earth now, one listening above the other to the same play following around the sunrise. Every one is affected by it—a kind of soul-suction—a great pulling from the world. People who do not want to write at all feel it—a kind of huge, soft, capillary attraction apparently—to a pen. The whole planet kindles every man's solitude. Continents are bellows for the glow in him if there is any. The wireless telegraph beckons ideas around the world. "How does a planet applaud?" dreams the young author. "With a faint flush of light?" One would like to be liked by it—speak one's little piece to it. When one was through, one could hear the soft hurrah through Space.

I wonder sometimes that in This Presence I ever could have thought or had times of thinking it was a little or a lonely world to write in—to flicker out thoughts in. When I think of what a world it was that came to men once and of the world that waits around me—around all of us now—I do like to mention it.

When many years ago, as a small boy, I was allowed for the first time to open the little inside door in the paddle-box of a great side-wheel steamer and watched its splendid thrust on the sea, I did not know why it was that I could not be called away from it, or why I stood and watched hour after hour unconscious before it—the thunder and the foam piling up upon my being. I have guessed now. I watch the drive-wheel of an engine now as if I were tracking out at last the last secret of loneliness. I face Time and Space with it. I know I have but to do a true deed and I am crowded round—to help me do it. I know I have but to think a true thought, but to be true and deep enough with a book—feel a worldful for it, put a worldful in it—and the whole planet will look over my shoulder while I write. Thousands of printing presses under a thousand skies I hear truth working softly, saying over and over, and around and around the earth, the word that was given to me to say.

Can any one believe that this strange new, deep, beautiful, clairvoyant feeling a man has nowadays every day, every hour, for the other side of a star, is not going to make arts and men and words and actions great in the world?

Silently, you and I, Gentle Reader, are watching the first great gathering-in of a world to listen and to live. The continents are unanimous. There has never been a quorum before. They are getting together at last for the first world-sized man, for the first world-sized word. They are listening him into life. It is really getting to be a planet now, a whole completed articulated, furnished, lived-through, loved-through star, from sun's end to sun's end. One sees the sign on it

TO LET

TO ANY MAN WHO REALLY WANTS IT.

VIII

THE IDEA OF LOVE AND COMRADESHIP

"Ever there comes an onward phrase to me

Of some transcendent music I have heard;

No piteous thing by soft hands dulcimered,

No trumpet crash of blood-sick victory.

But a glad strain of some still symphony

That no proud mortal touch has ever stirred."

Have you ever walked out over the hill in your city at night, Gentle Reader— your own city—felt the soul of it lying about you—lying there in its gentleness and splendor and lust? Have you never felt as you stood there that you had some right to it, some right way down in your being—that all this haze of light and darkness, all the people in it, somehow really belonged to you? We do not exactly let our souls say it—at least out loud—but there are times when I have been out in the street with The Others, when I have heard them—heard our souls, that is—all softly trooping through us, saying it to ourselves. "O to know—to be utterly known one moment; to have, if only for one second, twenty thousand souls for a home; to be gathered around by a city, to be sought out and haunted by some one great all-love, once, streets and silent houses of it!"

I go up and down the pavements reaching out into the days and nights of the men and the women. Perhaps you have seen me, Gentle Reader, in The Great Street, in the long, slow shuffle with the others? And I have said to you though I did not know it: "Did you not call to me? Did you hear anything? I think it was I calling to you."

I have sat at the feet of cities. I have swept the land with my soul. I have gone about and looked upon the face of the earth. I have demanded of smoking villages sweeping past and of the mountains and of the plains and of the middle of the sea: "Where are those that belong to me? Will I ever travel near enough, far enough?" I have gone up and down the world—seen the countless men and women in it, standing on either side of their Abyss of Circumstance, beckoning and reaching out. I have seen men and women sleepless, or worn, or old, casting their bread upon the waters, grasping at sunsets or afterglows, putting their souls like letters in bottles. Some of them seem to be flickering their lives out like Marconi messages into a sort of infinite, swallowing human space.

Always this same wild aimless sea of living. There does not seem to be a geography for love. My soul answered me: "Did you expect a world to be indexed? Life is steered by a Wind. Blossoms and cyclones and sunshine and you and I—all blundering along together." "Let every seed swell for itself," the Universe has said, in its first fine careless rapture. God is merely having a good time. Why should I go up and down a universe crying through it, "Where are those that belong to me?" I have looked at the stars swung out at me and they have not answered, and now when I look at the men, I have seemed to see them, every man in a kind of dull might, rushing, his hands before him, hinged on emptiness. "You are alone," the heart hath said. "Get up and be your own brother. The world is a great WHO CARES?"

But when, in the middle of deep, helpless sleep, tossed on the wide waters, I wake in a ship, feel it trembling all through out there with my brother's care for me, I know that this is not true. "Around sunsets, out through the great dark," I find myself saying, "he has reached over and held me. Out here on this high hill of water, under this low, touching sky, I sleep."

Sometimes I do not sleep. I lie awake silently, and feel gathered around. I wonder if I could be lonely if I tried. I touch the button by my pillow. I listen to great cities tending me. I have found all the earth paved, or carpeted, or hung, or thrilled through with my brother's thoughts for me. I cannot hide from love. He has hired oceans to do my errands. He has made the whole human race my house-servants. I lie in my berth for sheer joy, thinking of the strange peoples where the morning is, running to and fro for me, down under the dark. Next me, the great quiet throb of the engine—between me and infinite space—beating comfortably. I cannot help answering to it—this soft and mighty reaching out where I lie.

My thoughts follow along the great twin shafts my brother holds me with. I wonder about them. I wish to do and share with them.

Were I a spirit I would go

Where the murmuring axles of the screws

Along their whirling aisles

Break through the hold,

Where they lift the awful shining thews

Of Thought,

Of Trade,

And strike the Sea

Till the scar of London lies

Miles and miles upon its breast

Out in the West.

As I lie and look out of my port-hole and watch the starlight stepping along the sea I let my soul go out and visit with it. The ship I am in—a little human beckoning between two deserts. Out through my port-hole I seem to see other ships, ghosts of great cities—an ocean of them, creeping through their still huge picture of the night, with their low hoarse whistles meeting one another, whispering to one another under the stars.

"And they are all mine," I say, "hastening gently."

I lie awake thinking of it. I let my whole being float out upon the thought of it. The bare thought of it, to me, is like having lived a great life. It is as if I had been allowed to be a great man a minute. I feel rested down through to before I was born. The very stars, after it, seem rested over my head. I have gathered my universe about me. It is as if I had lain all still in my soul and some beautiful eternal sleep—a minute of it—had come to me and visited me. All men are my brothers. Is not the world filled with hastening to me?

What is there my brother has not done for me? From the uttermost parts of the morning, all things that are flow fresh and beautiful upon my flesh. He has laid my will on the heavens. His machines are like the tides that do not stop. They are a part of the vast antennæ of the earth. They have grown themselves upon it. Like wind and vapor and dust, they are a part of the furnishing of the earth. If I am cold and seek furs Alaska is as near as the next snowdrift. My brother has caused it to be so. Everywhere is five cents away. I take tea in Pekin with a spoon from Australia and a saucer from Dresden. With the handle of my knife from India and the blade from Sheffield, I eat meat from Kansas. Thousands of miles bring me spoonfuls. The taste in my mouth, five or six continents have made for me. The isles of the sea are on the tip of my tongue.

And this is the thing my brother means, the thing he has done for me, solitary. I keep saying it over to myself. I lie still and try to take it in—to feel the touch of the hands of his hands. Does any one say this thing he is doing is done for money—that it is not done for comradeship or love? Could money have thought of it or dared it or desired it? Could all the money in the world ever pay him for it? This paper-ticket I give him—for this berth I lie in—does it pay him for it? Do I think to pay my fare to the infinite?—I— a parasite of a great roar in a city? These seven nights in the hollow of his hand he has held me and let me look upon the heaped-up stillness in heaven—of clouds. I have visited with the middle of the sea.

And now with a thought, have I furnished my hot plain and smoke forever.

I have not time to dream. I spell out each night, before I sleep, some vast new far-off love, this new daily sense of mutual service, this whole round world to measure one's being against. Crowds wait on me in silence. I tip nations with a nickel. Who would believe it? I lie in my berth and laugh at the bigness of my heart.

When I go out on the meadow at high noon and in the great sleepy sunny silence there I stand and watch that long imperious train go by putting together the White Mountains and New York, it is no longer as it was at first, a mere train by itself to me,—a flash of parlor cars between a great city and a sky up on Mt. Washington. When it swings up between my two little mountains its huge banner of steam and smoke, it is the beckoning of The Other Trains, the whole starful, creeping through the Alps (that moment), stealing up the Andes, roaring through the sun or pounding through the dark on the under sides of the world.

In the great silence on the meadow after the train rolls by, it would be hard to be lonely for a minute, not to stand still, not to share in spirit around the earth a few of the big, happy things—the far unseen peoples in the sun, the streets, the domes and towers, the statesmen, and poets, but always between and above and beneath the streets and the domes and the towers, and the statesmen and poets—always the engineers,—I keep seeing them—these men who dip up the world in their hands, who sweep up life ... long, narrow, little towns of souls, and bowl them through the Days and Nights.

In this huge, bottomless, speechless, modern world—one would rather be running the poems than writing them. At night I turn in my sleep. I hear the midnight mail go by—that same still face before it, the great human headlight of it. I lie in my bed wondering. And when the thunder of the Face has died away, I am still wondering. Out there on the roof of the world, thundering alone, thundering past death, past glimmering bridges, past pale rivers, folding away villages behind him (the strange, soft, still little villages), pounding on the switch-lights, scooping up the stations, the fresh strips of earth and sky.... The cities swoon before him ... swoon past him. Thundering past his own thunder, echoes dying away ... and now out in the great plain, out in the fields of silence, drinking up mad splendid, little black miles.... Every now and then he thinks back over his shoulder, thinks back over his long roaring, yellow trail of souls. He laughs bitterly at sleep, at the men with tickets, at the way the men with tickets believe in him. He knows (he grips his hand on the lever) he is not infallible. Once ... twice ... he might have ... he almost.... Then suddenly there is a flash ahead ... he sets his teeth, he reaches out with his soul ... masters it, he strains himself up to his infallibility again ... all those people there ... fathers, mothers, children, ... sleeping on their arms full of dreams. He feels as the minister feels, I should think, when the bells have stopped on a Sabbath morning, when he stands in his pulpit alone, alone before God ... alone before the Great Silence, and the people bow their heads.

But I have found that it is not merely the machines that one can see at a glance are woven all through with men (like the great trains) which make the big companions. It is a mere matter of getting acquainted with the machines and there is not one that is not woven through with men, with dim faces of vanished lives—with inventors.

I have seen great wheels, in steam and in smoke, like swinging spirits of the dead. I have been told that the inventors were no longer with us, that their little tired, old-fashioned bodies were tucked in cemeteries, in the crypts of churches, but I have seen them with mighty new ones in the night—in the broad day, in a nameless silence, walk the earth. Inventors may not be put like engineers, in show windows in front of their machines, but they are all wrought into them. From the first bit of cold steel on the cowcatcher to the little last whiff of breath in the air-brake, they are wrought in—fibre of soul and fibre of body. As the sun and the wind are wrought in the trees and rivers in the mountains, they are there. There is not a machine anywhere, that has not its crowd of men in it, that is not full of laughter and hope and tears. The machines give one some idea, after a few years of listening, of what the inventors' lives were like. One hears them—the machines and the men, telling about each other.

There are days when it has been given to me to see the machines as inventors and prophets see them.

On these days I have seen inventors handling bits of wood and metal. I have seen them taking up empires in their hands and putting the future through their fingers.

On these days I have heard the machines as the voices of great peoples singing in the streets.

And after all, the finest and most perfect use of machinery, I have come to think, is this one the soul has, this awful, beautiful daily joy in its presence. To have this communion with it speaking around one, on sea and land, and in the low boom of cities, to have all this vast reaching out, earnest machinery of human life—sights and sounds and symbols of it, beckoning to one's spirit day and night everywhere, playing upon one the love and glory of the world—to have—ah, well, when in the last great moment of life I lay my universe out in order around about me, and lie down to die, I shall remember I have lived.

This great sorrowing civilization of ours, which I had seen before, always sorrowing at heart but with a kind of devilish convulsive energy in it, has come to me and lived with me, and let me see the look of the future in its face.

And now I dare look up. For a moment—for a moment that shall live forever—I have seen once, I think—at least once, this great radiant gesturing of Man around the edges of a world. I shall not die, now, solitary. And when my time shall come and I lie down to do it, oh, unknown faces that shall wait with me,—let it not be with drawn curtains nor with shy, quiet flowers of fields about me, and silence and darkness. Do not shut out the great heartless-sounding, forgetting-looking roar of life. Rather let the windows be opened. And then with the voice of mills and of the mighty street—all the din and wonder of it,—with the sound in my ears of my big brother outside living his great life around his little earth, I will fall asleep.

BIRD'S-EYE VIEW OF THIS BOOK

PART ONE

I. The word beautiful in 1905 is no longer shut in with its ancient rim of hills, or with a show of sunsets, or with bouquets and doilies and songs of birds. It is a man's word, says The Twentieth Century. "If a hill is beautiful. So is the locomotive that conquers a hill."

II. The modern literary man—slow to be converted, is already driven to his task. Living in an age in which nine-tenths of his fellows are getting their living out of machines, or putting their living into them, he is not content with a definition of beauty which shuts down under the floor of the world nine tenths of his fellowbeings, leaves him standing by himself with his lonely idea of beauty, where—except by shouting or by looking down through a hatchway he has no way of communing with his kind.

III. Unless he can conquer the machines, interpret them for the soul or the manhood of the men about him he sees that after a little while—in the great desert of machines, there will not be any men. A little while after that there will not be any machines. He has come to feel that the whole problem of civilization turns on it—on what seems at first sight an abstract or literary theory—that there is poetry in machines. If we cannot find a great hope or a great meaning for the machine-idea in its simplest form, the machines of steel and flame that minister to us, if inspiring ideas cannot be connected with a machine simply because it is a machine, there is not going to be anything left in modern life with which to connect inspiring ideas. All our great spiritual values are being operated as machines. To take the stand that inspiring ideas and emotions can be and will be connected with machinery is to take a stand for the continued existence of modern religion (in all reverence) the God-machine, for modern education, the man-machine, for modern government, the crowd-machine, for modern art, the machine that expresses the crowd, and for modern society—the machine in which the crowd lives.

IV. V. The poetry in machinery is a matter of fact. The literary men who know the men who know the machines, the men who live with them, the inventors, and engineers and brakemen have no doubts about the poetry in machinery. The real problem that stands in the way of interpreting and bringing out the poetry in machinery, instead of being a literary or æsthetic problem is a social one. It is in getting people to notice that an engineer is a gentleman and a poet.

VI. The inventor is working out the passions and the freedoms of the people, the tools of the nations.

The people are already coming to look upon the inventor under our modern conditions as the new form of prophet. If what we call literature cannot interpret the tools that men are daily doing their living with, literature as a form of art, is doomed. So long as men are more creative and godlike in engines than they are in poems the world listens to engines. If what we call the church cannot interpret machines, the church as a form of religion loses its leadership until it does. A church that can only see what a few of the men born in an age, are for, can only help a few. A religion that lives in a machine-age and that does not see and feel the meaning of that age, is not worthy of us. It is not even worthy of our machines. One of the machines that we have made could make a better religion than this.

PART TWO

THE LANGUAGE OF THE MACHINES

I. I have heard it said that if a thing is to be called poetic it must have great ideas in it and must successfully express them; that the language of the machines, considered as an expression of the ideas that are in the machines, is irrelevant and absurd. But all language looked at in the outside way that men have looked at machines, is irrelevant and absurd. We listen solemnly to the violin, the voice of an archangel with a board tucked under his chin. Except to people who have tried it, nothing could be more inadequate than kissing as a form of human expression, between two immortal infinite human beings.

II. The chief characteristic of the modern machine as well as of everything else that is strictly modern is that it refuses to show off. The man who is looking at a twin-screw steamer and who is not feeling as he looks at it the facts and the ideas that belong with it, is not seeing it. The poetry is under water.

III. I have heard it said that the modern man does not care for poetry. It would be truer to say that he does not care for old-fashioned poetry—the poetry that bears on. The poetry in a Dutch windmill flourishes and is therefore going by, to the strictly modern man. The idle foolish look of a magnet appeals to him more. Its language is more expressive and penetrating. He has learned that in proportion as a machine or anything else is expressive—in the modern language, it hides. The more perfect or poetic he makes his machines the more spiritual they become. His utmost machines are electric. Electricity is the modern man's prophet. It sums up his world. It has the modern man's temperament—the passion of being invisible and irresistible.

IV. Poetry and religion consist—at bottom, in being proud of God. Most men to-day are worshipping God—at least in secret, not merely because of this great Machine that He has made, running softly above us—moonlight and starlight ... but because He has made a Machine that can make machines, a machine that shall take more of the dust of the earth and of the vapor of heaven and crowd it into steel and iron and say "Go ye now,—depths of the earth, heights of heaven—serve ye me! Stones and mists, winds and waters and thunder—the spirit that is in thee is my spirit. I also, even I also am God!"

V. Everything has its language and the power of feeling what a thing means, by the way it looks, is a matter of noticing, of learning the language. The language of the machines is there. I cannot precisely know whether the machines are expressing their ideas or not. I only know that when I stand before a foundry hammering out the floors of the world, clashing its awful cymbals against the night, I lift my soul to it, and in some way—I know not how, while it sings to me, I grow strong and glad.

PART THREE

THE MACHINES AS POETS

I. II. Machinery has poetry in it because it expresses the soul of man—of a whole world of men.

It has poetry in it because it expresses the individual soul of the individual man who creates the Machine—the inventor, and the man who lives with the machine—the engineer.

It has poetry in it because it expresses God. He is the kind of God who can make men who can make machines.

III. IV. Machinery has poetry in it because in expressing the man's soul it expresses the greatest idea that the soul of man can have—the man's sense of being related to the Infinite. It has poetry in it not merely because it makes the man think he is infinite but because it is making the man as infinite as he thinks he is. When I hear the machines, I hear Man saying, "God and I."

V. Machinery has poetry in it because in expressing the infinity of man it expresses the two great immeasurable ideas of poetry and of the imagination and of the soul in all ages—the two forms of infinity—the liberty and the unity of man.

The substance of a beautiful thing is its Idea.

A beautiful thing is beautiful in proportion as its form reveals the nature of its substance, that is, conveys its idea.

Machinery is beautiful by reason of immeasurable ideas consummately expressed.

PART FOUR

THE IDEAS BEHIND THE MACHINES

The ideas of machinery in their several phases are sketched in chapters as follows:

I. II. The idea of the incarnation. The God in the body of the man.

III. The idea of liberty—the soul's rescue from environment.

IV. The idea of immortality.

V. The idea of God.

VI. The idea of the Spirit—of the Unseen and Intangible.

VII. The practical idea of invoking great men.

VIII. The religious idea of love and comradeship.

Note.—The present volume is the first of a series which had their beginnings in some articles in the *Atlantic* a few years ago, answering or trying to answer the question, "Can a machine age have a soul?" Perhaps it is only fair to the present conception, as it stands, to suggest that it is an overture, and that the various phases and implications of machinery—the general bearing of machinery in our modern life, upon democracy, and upon the humanities and the arts, are being considered in a series of three volumes called:

I. The Voice of the Machines.

II. Machines and Millionaires.

III. Machines and Crowds.

www.ingramcontent.com/pod-product-compliance
Ingram Content Group UK Ltd.
Pitfield, Milton Keynes, MK11 3LW, UK
UKHW042150281224
453045UK00004B/307

9 789362 993359